Early Sunday Morning

★★★

The Pearl Harbor Diary of Amber Billows

BY BARRY DENENBERG

Scholastic Inc. New York

Washington, D.C.
1941

✪✪✪

Monday, October 20, 1941
Washington, D.C.

When Daddy tapped his fork on his water glass
last night and announced (in his usual, upbeat
fashion) that he had "exciting news for the entire
Billows family" (he always refers to us as "the
Billows family," as if we were one of his favorite
radio shows), everyone knew what was coming
next. We might as well start packing.

We were moving — yet again — and the only
question was where and when.

Equally certain was that the next sentence
would be (which it was): "Who can guess where
we're headed?" — which Dad says in a way that
makes you think he had four, first-class train tick-
ets to heaven tucked safe and sound in his back

pocket. (Dad's kind of a positive thinker. Some-one else's problems are his golden opportunities. Fortunately, Mom's not-so-sunny disposition provides the necessary balance. She's not nearly as upbeat as Dad. For her, disaster is lurking around every corner.)

I could see that this time even Mom didn't know where we were going.

Dad insists everyone be *really, really* serious about their guesses. If you blurt out the first thing that comes to your mind, just to get it over with, he'll get that disappointed look on his face that only prolongs the process, so everyone concentrates real hard.

Mom guessed (hopefully) back to Boston because, for one thing, that's where she was born, and for another, it's where Grandma and Grandpa live.

Dad didn't say anything, so I knew it wasn't Boston. If it was, he would have told her right away, before me and Andy, because it would have made her *so* happy. I had the feeling wherever we were going wasn't going to make her that happy.

Andy guessed St. Louis, but that's just because they have a National League team there — a team that would play his beloved Brooklyn Dodgers. (He's still recovering from the Dodgers winning their first pennant in twenty years and then losing the World Series to the Yankees because the catcher dropped the ball, or something like that.)

After Andy, Dad gave me his I-will-not-reveal-our-true-destination-until-everyone-has-guessed look, so the pressure was really on.

Like Mom, I, too, wished we were going back to Boston, but since Mom had already guessed that (Dad hates it when you guess the same city) and I knew it wasn't Boston I decided to pick a long shot: San Francisco. That really perked up the crowd, who got even more perked when Dad, obviously delighted with my effort, said, "Close, very close," and he paused, basking in the spotlight of our startled stares.

"Hawaii," he said. "We're going to Hawaii."

Now I think if you would have given each of us a million guesses, Hawaii would have been number one million and one on each of our lists.

First of all, the last time I looked, Hawaii wasn't even in the United States. I didn't know where it was and I could tell by the looks on their faces that neither did Mom or Andy.

Fortunately, Mom had the good sense to ask the question that was on everyone's mind: When?

"Next week," Dad said, as if it were the greatest news in the world.

That's when I had the fit.

It all came out.

I told Dad I didn't ever remember starting school in September like everyone else. I told him how horrible it was: being escorted to my homeroom by the principal; standing there and being introduced to an entire room of strange faces, knowing mine must have been turning as red as the stripes on the flag hanging over my head; pretending that everyone in the class wasn't really staring at me and that my glasses couldn't have been fogging up that badly; praying that at least one girl didn't think I was the biggest fool she ever saw in her life.

Now that the dam had burst, it was too late to hold back.

I told him how it takes me a year just to figure out the bus trip, where the classrooms are, which kids to avoid, and which teachers (if any) I could trust.

And how by the time I get ever-so-slightly settled in, it's time to move to the next city.

All I asked was that we move in the summer, like everyone else. There were families whose dads got transferred places but they did it over the summer, in an orderly fashion. Not next week.

Sometimes, I said, certain that this would be news to him, they even went to see the city first. They looked for a nice place to live. They saw what the schools were like. Sometimes just the moms went, and sometimes just the dads. And sometimes the entire family.

But they always, always did the actual, physical moving over the summer because it made everything so much easier for everyone. The packing, the moving, the going, the arriving, and most important (and here I had the feeling someone was actually screaming), SO THAT THE CHILDREN COULD START SCHOOL ON THE SAME DAY AS EVERYONE ELSE.

Then I ran to my room (which is in the basement), ran into my closet, slammed the door, sat on the floor, and chewed my bottom lip because I had sworn I was going to stop chewing my nails down to the quick every time we moved.

I was so angry, I forgot to cry.

When Mom knocked on the closet door and whispered that she wanted to talk, I knew I was a goner. (Whispering might be fine for other people, but coming from Mom it was a bad sign. It meant she was at her most, most serious.)

For some reason, which I can't quite figure out, I don't like to fight with Mom. It just isn't any fun. She never yells, never loses her temper, and never says anything she has to be sorry for later. It's really awful.

She's always very serious about it. Mom doesn't like it when anyone in the family disagrees with anyone else in the family, and when it happens she won't let up until the offending family member SEES THE ERROR OF THEIR WAYS. You don't even have to apologize, you just have to SEE THE ERROR OF YOUR WAYS. I *hate* seeing the error of my ways.

Fortunately, Mom gets to the point a whole lot quicker than Dad. She said that no one hated how much we had to move more than Dad. And that he hated it even more that we had to move at the drop of a hat (Mom and Dad are about equal on the corny expression meter).

But, she said, looking at me with the serious stare she has, that's one of the sacrifices your

9

father has to make if he wants to be a good re-porter. I'd had enough, but Mom wasn't finished. She explained that, besides his family, being a good newspaper reporter was the most important thing in Dad's life and that we were lucky to have a father who loved what he did and would I want him to do something he didn't like just so we didn't have to move, till I wanted to shout, "STOP, STOP, STOP," which I did, although I didn't shout it, I just said it.

We shook hands, which is one of the things Mom insists we do after a disagreement.

I was still mad, though, and decided to stay in my room, even though I knew that would make Dad sad.

I couldn't help it.

★★★

Tuesday, October 21, 1941
Washington, D.C.

I decided I wasn't mad at Daddy anymore because I was so mad at Andy. I'm the only one who *ever* says anything about moving. The one thing Andy does complain about is that we never live in a city that has a National League team. Dad told him that cities like Philadelphia, Milwaukee, and Cincinnati don't have much going on, so his paper doesn't want him to live there. Andy said that Hawaii was a new low for us because they don't have any baseball teams at all. At least it was something. But as long as there's a ball, a bat, and a glove somewhere, Andy doesn't care where we live. (He doesn't have trouble making friends, like I do.)

He's afraid to say anything to Daddy. Daddy's his hero. Andy wants to be a reporter just like him. (Although he likes to say "journalist." He told me it sounds more distinguished. He hasn't figured out yet that "Andy" is about the most undistinguished first name you can have.)

Andy thinks being fifteen is a big achievement and because I'm three years younger than him I should worship the ground he walks on.

He's right about one thing, though. There is a silver lining to this dark cloud: At least we won't have to live in Washington anymore. *Everyone* hates Washington: Andy, because the Dodgers don't play here; me, because of the long, hot summers and the long, cold winters.

Even Dad hates it, although he won't admit it. Mom hates it more than any of us. She says that everyone in Washington spends every waking minute thinking up what to lie about next. (Dad says Mom "doesn't suffer fools gladly." I'm not sure what that means, but if it means she doesn't stand for anyone's nonsense, he's right.)

When Daddy announces that we're moving, I begin a brand-new diary. (It makes me feel better.) So far I have three. There's my Washington diary, my Boston diary, and my back-to-Washington diary. By the time I'm done I suppose I'll have about a million.

We've lived in Washington, Boston, Baltimore, and New York City. New York is where I was born, but I don't remember much about that because we moved when I was two.

Andy says New York was the best because he liked living in an apartment more than a house. There were lots of kids in the building, and Mom didn't have to do all the things with the house that drive her nuts.

My favorite place was Boston. We lived right near the Boston Public Garden, which is the best place on earth. I wish we had never had to leave.

Andy says Dad took him to a Dodgers game when we lived in New York, but he doesn't remember it too well.

The only time I was ever in New York, besides when I was born, was two years ago, when we all went to the World's Fair.

I had such a good time. I can still picture the parachute jump. The parachutes were red and white, with yellow, red, and green Life Savers on the top. They were like collapsed umbrellas on the way up and opened ones on the way down.

Mom and I went up in one chute, and Daddy and Andy in another. We were hundreds of feet up in the air — so high, you could see the whole fair and all the teeny-tiny people scurrying around down below.

It felt like it took forever to get up to the top. (Dad told us later it only takes forty-two seconds, and that when you go down it's like falling off a twenty-story building.) The ten seconds it took to come down made me lose my breath. (Mom said it almost made her lose her lunch.)

We went on all sorts of other rides, took a bus around the whole fair, and saw the General Motors Futurama exhibit, where they showed what the future would be like in the year 1960 (so far away, who could even imagine it?). They had a car with a transparent plastic body so you could see how it worked, and this strange new thing called "television," which was like radio with a picture.

At the end we got a button that said: I HAVE SEEN THE FUTURE.

The only problem was that you had to stand in line for pretty much everything, and it was really, really hot. My feet were aching, so I took off my shoes and dangled my feet in this big pool with a nice fountain, and Dad said not to do that but then he and Mom looked at each other, started to laugh, took off their shoes, and dangled them in, too.

Wednesday, October 22, 1941
Washington, D.C.

As soon as I told Allison we were moving, she got mad, which was not at all the response I was expecting. I told her it wasn't my fault we were moving, and she said it was. She said I told her when we first became best friends (in the middle of last year) that I didn't think we would be moving for a while because (thanks to the war) there was all sorts of good stuff for my dad to report on right here in Washington. I only said that because that's what Mom told me.

I tried to explain that the war might be spreading. That it might not just be in Europe anymore but all over because of Japan. (Although I'm not 100 percent sure what Japan has to do with all of it.)

I was hoping this would make her less angry, but I could see that it wasn't, because the tears were just streaming down her face and she walked away even before I could finish, which wasn't very nice.

★★★

Thursday, October 23, 1941
Washington, D.C.

I spent all yesterday afternoon in the library reading about Hawaii.

It's a territory of the United States, I discovered. I didn't know the United States had territories. I didn't know we had anything besides the forty-eight states.

And it's not one thing, it's lots and lots of things — islands, almost a hundred of them.

It's even farther away than I'd thought: 2,390 miles from the coast of California.

It sounds like it's in the middle of nowhere.

They used to be called the Sandwich Islands, in honor of the same guy they named the sandwich after. He must have been a big deal to have a whole place named after him and a meal.

The name Hawaii means "paradise," and from the pictures, the islands do look pretty.

They have exotic fish and exotic-sounding

tropical plants whose names I can't even pronounce: bougainvillea, hibiscus, jacaranda, algaroba.

It's hot and dry in summer (what a relief that will be) and about 70 degrees morning, noon, and night, 365 days of the year, so they don't wear a lot of clothes because it's spring all year-round.

We're going to live near Honolulu, which is on one of the larger islands. There's a really nice beach there called Waikiki, and the beach boys surf the waves. It's near Pearl Harbor, which is where the U.S. Navy parks its boats, at least according to Mr. Military (my brother).

He assures me, as if I really cared, that there are battleships, destroyers, and aircraft carriers there. He's excited because Dad said he knew an admiral or two who can take us for a ride.

Hawaii doesn't sound like it's very American, though. Once it was ruled by a queen whose name was Lili something. And I read that if you were found standing in a position that was higher than the king's, you would be put to death. When the king was inspecting a ship and decided to go below, everyone had to dive overboard so that they would be below him and therefore avoid execution.

That's not the only bad news.

There are volcanoes that are active (which means, I think, that they work) and earthquakes. There are so many volcanoes that they have to have their own personal goddess, Pele.

I thought volcanoes and earthquakes were extinct, like dinosaurs. Or, if they weren't extinct, at least they were far, far away, so you didn't have to worry about them. Of course, Hawaii is far, far away.

From the pictures and what I read I don't think the people there look like me. They look very, very tan and have long, black hair. They're Polynesian (whatever that is), Japanese, Chinese, and from places I've never even heard of: Korea, Vietnam, and Cambodia.

They don't even speak English there. They do,

but they speak other things, too (like Hawaiian). It'll be just great if I have to learn another language and, instead of taking math in English, which is plenty hard enough, I'll have to take it in Hawaiian.

Andy's right. It's like we're moving to another planet.

Friday, October 24, 1941
Washington, D.C.

I talked to Mom about Hawaii while she was preparing The Last Dinner Party.

She says we will be able to cook some really exotic food, like stone-cooked pig.

Mom loves to cook more than almost anything in the world, and she's really, really good at it. She read about the stone-cooked pig in one of the books I brought home from the library. Unfortunately, it explained precisely what you do.

You kill the pig the night before, dip it in some really, really hot water, take out the insides, rub the outside with salt, and hang it up overnight. (Mom read all this to me like it was "sauté until golden brown and turn over.")

Then in the morning you dig this really gigantic pit, make this really gigantic fire, put rocks on top of the wood, and then hot rocks inside the poor pig. Then you cover everything with dirt and ashes from the fire, cook for two hours, and serve with sweet potatoes and yams.

Yummy.

Mom's really looking forward to going to Hawaii. She thinks it will be nice and quiet and that it will be nice for all of us to take it easy for a while. I think she means that it's going to be good for Dad to get away from all the hubbub in Washington.

And, course, there's the new baby.

The baby's due in May. Mom says she doesn't

care if it's a boy or a girl, but I think she wants a girl. It better be a girl.

Saturday, October 25, 1941
Washington, D.C.

I can't believe Mom and Dad are having a dinner party tomorrow night when we're leaving in just four days. Luckily, for the first time, we don't have to pack everything ourselves. Dad's paper is having a moving company come in and do it for us. Mom says that's because Dad's a pretty big deal now, which is only right, given how hard he works and how much he cares.

I hope he has a nicer office than the one he has here, which is so small that he has to pile everything all over the place.

Of course Dad insists on packing his books himself. Dad takes great pride in his library, and I think a lot of the books are old and fragile and he's afraid to let the moving men do it.

I don't know why they are called dinner "parties" rather than just plain "dinner." There really isn't a party, just lots of smoking, drinking, eating, and talking. Talking is the whole reason we have so many dinner parties. (Besides the fact that Mom loves to show off her cooking skills. No matter what city we're living in, everyone's always pleased to get an invitation to one of Mom's dinner parties. I think she has some kind of reputation or something.)

That's how Dad gets a lot of his information. "Background," he calls it. He's real serious about things like politics and world affairs, especially lately.

Dad's a real master at getting his guests to do all the talking. To me it's kind of obvious, but maybe that's just because I know how he operates.

First there're the cocktails.

Dad mixes the drinks and makes sure the martinis are very dry and the bourbon is very old-fashioned. I don't understand the very "dry" part, but I think the "old-fashioned" part means that there are lots of cherries and pieces of orange in it.

Mom shows the ladies around the house and conducts what she calls "girl talk": cooking, clothes, the neighborhood, school, and stuff like that, none of which (other than cooking) actually interests Mom. That way, Dad can concentrate on the guys and the small-talk segment.

During the small-talk segment, Dad will do plenty of talking as long as it's about nothing much like sports, cars, sports cars, and the weather.

He talks so much, you begin to think he's a pretty forthright guy, willing to talk about anything under the sun. It kind of gets you in the mood, helped by what Dad calls "the universal lubricant," alcohol. Of course no one ever notices that all Dad ever drinks is seltzer. He doesn't like alcohol; he says it clouds the mind. Dad likes to keep his mind very uncloudy.

When we were younger, Mom would give me and Andy dinner first. Then, when the guests arrived and they saw how tall we were (although Andy's pretty much a shrimp), we would go up to our rooms for the rest of the evening. Now that we're older they let us eat with them, which can be pretty boring. But I think it would hurt Dad's feelings if I said I would like to eat first and spend the night reading in my room.

By the time everyone's sat down to dinner, having had a drink or two, Dad delivers a line like: "I don't know, the whole thing just confuses the hell out of me, Senator (or General), and I'd really like to hear your views on the matter," and that's pretty much all they need. They're off and running, blabbing away, pausing only briefly to praise Mom's Coq au Vin or Veal Cordon Bleu, and then it's back to Roosevelt, Hitler, Churchill, and Mussolini.

After dessert, coffee, cigars, and brandy, Mom and Dad, like two little tugboats, ferry their bloated guests toward the front door, where Dad invariably has to say, "Here's your coat and hat, what's your hurry."

We're having an isolationist to dinner tomorrow night. The reason I know is Mom's making meat loaf, mashed potatoes, and apple pie. Mom says that isolationists are so American that that's all they eat for every single meal, which I find hard to believe. (Sometimes you don't know whether or not to believe some of the things Mom says. Dad says she has a very dry sense of humor, like a martini, I guess.) Even if you're an isolationist you must get bored eating meat loaf, mashed potatoes, and apple pie for every single meal.

Mom says isolationists live in a dream world and they may be kidding themselves but they're not kidding her. She especially hates Charles Lindbergh, even though the rest of the world loves him. Mom says he's the King of the Isolationists and just because he knows how to fly an airplane, everyone listens to what he has to say. Mom says if he didn't have that deceptively boyish grin, no one would care so much about what he had to say.

She doesn't call him the Lone Eagle; she calls him the Lone Ostrich, because that's what Walter Winchell, her favorite radio commentator, calls him. (Mom hardly ever misses his program. I love the way it begins: "Good evening, Mr. and Mrs. North America and all the ships at sea.") Lindbergh is trying to convince everyone that the war in Europe is not something we should get involved in, that it need only concern England, France, Germany, and Russia. It's their war, not ours, Lindbergh says. We don't have to worry, because we have the gigantic Atlantic Ocean protecting us like a moat that surrounds a castle. That's why Mom calls him the King of the Isolationists, because he acts like he's the king and the United States is his castle. Mom thinks he wants to be president someday.

She thinks that what Lindbergh is saying is utter nonsense.

I'm not sure what Dad thinks, although he knows enough not to say anything good about Lindbergh in front of Mom. He seems more concerned lately and talks about "the dire state of the world"; "darkening clouds on the horizon"; and "leaving us no choice" more and more frequently.

We'll see if Mom pulls her "scalding soup attack" trick tomorrow night. If Mom doesn't like someone, she makes sure their bowl of soup is about a billion degrees Fahrenheit. Then, when they take the first spoonful, she waits to see them wince in pain and says (in her most sincere manner), "I hope the soup's hot enough for everyone," carefully avoiding looking at her victim.

✪✪✪

Sunday, October 26, 1941
Washington, D.C.

Mom and Dad got into an argument after dinner, which is a rare occurrence. They don't usually argue — I'm not saying they *never* argue, but it's rare and when they do, it's BEHIND CLOSED DOORS. They don't even raise their voices, so it's impossible to hear what they're saying even if you put a glass to the wall. (Frankly, I think that's a big waste of time. All it does is make your ears red.)

The argument began while Dad and I were helping clear the dessert dishes, coffee cups, and ashtrays from the dining room table. (Andy, who is unbelievably lazy and gets away with it because he's a boy, was already up in his room.)

Dad always helps Mom with the dishes, even drying them and putting them away. (He doesn't like to wash, because that makes his fingers wrinkle and he has trouble typing his articles. When he says this, Mom calls him Mr. Hunt and Peck.)

I'm a great eavesdropper. I do it at school with the teachers all the time. It's all in where and how you stand. You can't be face-to-face or even back-to-back (too obvious). You just have to stand sort of sideways *and* off to the side. Just far enough away so they don't notice you're near them but close enough to hear what's being said. You don't need to be so close you can hear every single word. Don't be greedy — that's the key.

The funny thing about the argument was that there's a swinging door connecting the dining room and the kitchen, so Dad would be taking some plates into the kitchen and I would hear him up to when he went through the door and then as he came back out I would hear him and Mom until the door swung closed and then I could just hear him and not Mom, so I couldn't really make out everything but I caught most of it.

One of the guests at dinner was Senator Mucky Muck. (That's not his real name — I can never remember his real name — that's just what Dad says. Dad says he's a "real big mucky muck." I call his wife Mrs. Mouse because she's so teeny tiny and never says a word. Boy, does she wear a lot of perfume. The only time she ever utters a sound is when she wants her martini "freshened," as she puts it. Mom said that she recently recovered from a complete nervous breakdown. I'd like to have seen her before she recovered.)

Mom was mad because Dad didn't say anything in response to Senator Mucky Muck's views. Senator Mucky Muck is an isolationist. (I noticed that he gobbled up all his meat loaf and mashed potatoes and asked for seconds on both. Maybe Mom is right.)

Dad gets even more patient than usual when Mom gets like this, which is a good idea, I can tell you from experience.

He explained to her that the entire purpose of the dinner party was to find out what important people in government were thinking, so he could

SERVE HIS READERSHIP PROPERLY. (This is a very serious phrase for Dad and one of the few things you can't joke about.)

Mom, who, of course, knows all this, said she was willing to listen to most anything but this "isolationist garbage." She said that she didn't have any readership to serve (I thought Mom was getting awful close to crossing the line here) and she wasn't sitting still for it anymore. The next time, she was going to speak her mind.

She told Dad he was "duly warned." Dad looked "duly warned."

Monday, October 27, 1941
Washington, D.C.

I wasn't going to talk to Allison even if she talked to me, but she didn't. I had to be with her every day in every class for all of last week, pretending every single minute that she didn't exist.

Mom was right. I should have more than

one friend. Mom thinks it would be better if I had two or three friends or even a group of friends, but I don't like that. I like to have just one best friend I can depend on. As soon as I move to a city I find someone to have as a best friend and that's it.

It's too complicated having more than one friend. But Mom says that sometimes having more friends can be less complicated.

I wish I had listened to her, because now I dread going to school because I don't have anyone else besides Sylvia Prescott to be friends with. Sylvia's nice and pretty much worships me, which is kind of the problem because she's a little boring.

I don't see why I have to go to school, anyway. We're leaving soon for Hawaii, so what does it matter? I'll just be missing a couple of days more.

Mom just laughed when I said that. She's even more serious than Dad about school.

There seems to be an endless list of things to

do, and everyone's running around, bumping into one another like balls on a pool table.

I have to figure out what I'm going to be taking, because Mom says we're going to stay in a hotel until our stuff comes. I have absolutely no idea what all the kids in Hawaii will be wearing. I am definitely taking my shaggy sweaters, even though I know it's really warm there. I took my pleated skirts, including my two houndstooth ones, the black and white and the brownish one, and all my kneesocks. I wonder if they wear kneesocks in Hawaii.

I've been so busy, I haven't had time to properly concentrate on how terrified I am of going on my first airplane flight.

Andy said it's nothing and then started telling me everything I never wanted to know about air travel. Of course I don't know how he would really know since he's never been in a plane, either.

I don't know why my first flight has to be a thousand hours long.

Mom said I should make sure I bring enough books to read on the airplane. I don't know how much is enough, but I'm bringing two Nancy Drews — *The Secret of the Old Clock* and *The Bungalow Mystery* — *The Little House in the Big Woods* and *The Yearling*. That should last me for a while.

After dinner I was in my room looking at this picture book of Hawaii that I took out of the library. There was a knock on the door. Our family has a strict door-knocking policy. Dad's a big believer in privacy — his and everyone else's (which is odd for someone whose job is basically to snoop on other people, but I've never said that to him).

If you're in your room with the door closed, no one can enter under any circumstances (unless it's a real emergency) until the person inside says it's okay. We do a lot of knocking, and you come to recognize everyone's knock.

Andy's is boomboomboom, three knocks right in a row with no space at all in between, like he's going to crash down the door if you don't answer right away. Dad's knock is also three, but it's more a tap, tap, tap. Very polite and patient, like Dad. Mom and I are both two knocks. Mine's knock, k-n-o-c-k, one short and one long, and Mom's knock, knock, simple and to the point.

So when I heard knock, knock I was sure it was Mom and said, come in.

I was shocked when I looked up from my book and Allison was standing at the foot of my bed.

She looked so stricken that I forgot to act like I was mad, which I kind of was but I kind of wasn't. I thought maybe something had happened to her father, who has been in and out of the hospital, although Allison doesn't know why. No one in her family will tell her. Allison's family doesn't like to talk about *anything*. They give me the creeps, although I never say anything to Allison, because I think they give her the creeps, too, and if I said anything it would just make her feel even worse.

That's why she loves to spend so much time with my family and which is why Mom let her come right up to my room. At least I think that's why.

Before I could even ask her what was the matter, she said she would like to start the conversation about my moving to Hawaii over again, from the beginning, which I thought was a good idea. But when I said that we were moving to Hawaii, she just started crying again and said she would miss me so much, she could hardly bear to think about it and that she would never find a better best friend, ever.

I really hate it when people cry and I really hate it when they say something nice to you. I don't think it's one of my better characteristics. (As a matter of fact it might be my worst.) It makes me feel really, really embarrassed, and when it happens I act really strangely.

So I started to laugh.

I was just trying to cheer Allison up. I told her I would write once a week no matter what and that I was the most reliable pen pal, which isn't at all true, as Allison knows (when she went to Maine for the summer, I didn't answer a single one of her letters), but which was such an outrageous lie that it actually made her start laughing and I knew that was my chance and I asked her if she wanted to go downstairs and have ice cream with my mom and dad. Having ice cream with my mom and dad is one of Allison's favorite things to do. Mom and Dad are always counting calories (Dad's a little on the plump side of things, and Mom's been extra careful ever since the baby), but after-dinner-before-bed-ice-cream is a family ritual.

Fortunately we were distracted over ice cream because Andy's still upset that Daddy has to sell the Chevrolet. The one with the nifty gadget that squirts clean water onto the windshield when you press a button. Dad told Andy he could help him pick out the new car when we get to Hawaii, but I don't know if that helped.

Andy wants to learn to speak Hawaiian (not that he's doing that well with English), and so he's practicing. *Aloha* means "welcome," "love," or "farewell"; *mahalo* means "thanks." We will be *mahinis*, which is "newcomers," and I'm a *wahine*, which is "girl."

So I guess it's so long, Washington, D.C., and *aloha*, Oahu, Hawaii.

Oahu, Hawaii

⭐⭐⭐

Friday, November 7, 1941
Oahu, Hawaii

The flight from Washington to San Francisco took forever, and the flight from San Francisco to Hawaii took forever and a day (over eighteen hours). I must say it was pretty exciting and not as scary as I thought it would be.

At San Francisco we boarded the *China Clipper,* which is a flying boat — it's like a really, really big motorboat with a giant wing on top of it. We took off from a floating pier and landed on the water. The four huge propellers are way high up so they don't get dunked in the water. When we landed we putt-putted up to the pier.

We left at 3:00 P.M. and arrived in Honolulu 9:00 A.M. the next day. I slept a lot of the time (the San Francisco to Hawaii part is half overnight).

I'm a pretty good sleeper, especially when we travel anywhere. When we're in the car I lay my head on Andy's lap and I'm sound asleep in five minutes.

I read almost all of the books I brought and did crossword puzzles. We played Information Please, Monopoly (for three hours — Mom won), and then tried to see if all of us together could name the capitals of all forty-eight states. We couldn't. No one knew the capital of Michigan (Lansing) or Kentucky (Frankfort).

Dinner was quite elegant (Mom was *really* impressed). It was served in the dining lounge and the tables were beautifully set with white linen tablecloths, sparkling silverware, and very pretty china plates.

Now I know where the sun was all the time we lived in Washington, right here in Hawaii. Andy's right, this is another planet. A planet where they only have nice weather. It was 78 degrees the day we arrived (and it's been that way every day since) — 78 degrees in November! The air even *smells* different: clean and sweet. Mom says that's because of the ocean.

She thinks the climate will be good for Andy's asthma. Sometimes his attacks are so bad, he has to get under a kind of tent and inhale mentholated steam so he can breathe.

We went to the beach at Waikiki. There are *actually* beach boys there who surf the waves. They have really good tans and lots of muscles. There were supposed to be boys who dive off the piers and swim out for the coins the tourists throw in the water, but I didn't see them.

Dad says that if you give the surfers some money, they will take you for a ride. I don't think I'm quite ready for that yet, thanks to my brother.

Andy said there used to be twice as many surfers (as if he would know — Andy has to pretend he knows *everything*), but the rest were eaten by sharks. Sharks eat so many surfers because turtles are their favorite food and when they look up and see someone paddling on a surfboard, they think it's a turtle and accidentally eat them.

Unfortunately he succeeded in getting me completely nuts about the sharks (not that it took that much), and I've crossed surfing off my Top Ten list of things to do while in Hawaii.

I wish we could have stayed at the hotel longer. The Royal Hawaiian Hotel is the prettiest hotel I've ever seen. It's coral pink, and there are panoramic views of the towering mountains poking their peaks up through the clouds. The whole island seems to be bright green except for the turquoise sea and the blue sky.

We had breakfast brought up to the room, and one day I had waffles and the next sliced papaya, Portuguese sausage, and eggs (none of which, except for the eggs, I had ever had before).

I really, really like my new bedroom. It's sunny and airy and much bigger than any bedroom I ever had before. Of course, the whole house is about twice as big as any house we ever lived in.

There are three bedrooms and three bathrooms, so that we can each have our own. (In Washington and Boston I had to share a bathroom with Andy, which is one of the worst experiences imaginable.)

Mom's spent the past forty-eight hours organizing the kitchen. (She's trying to get ready for Thanksgiving.) We both think the kitchen is the prettiest room in the house because it has this big bay window that lets in the morning sunlight.

Dad said I can paint my room lavender (which is my favorite color). As much as I liked living in the hotel, it's nice to be sleeping in my own bed again.

Sunday, November 9, 1941
Oahu, Hawaii

Now I know the real reason Dad was transferred to Hawaii. It was so he could play more golf. Of course, according to him it's *strictly* business. He claims it's even better than dinner parties for getting the "inside story."

Dad likes to do a lot of what he calls "socializing" and Mom calls "schmoozing." (I think there's a big difference.) Besides her dinner parties (which, frankly, she does mostly for Dad's sake), Mom's pretty much a loner. The only social activity Mom really likes is playing hearts. Mom likes to play hearts (even more than she likes to listen to Benny Goodman).

She tried to teach me to play, but I'm not real good at card games (or any kind of games, now that I think of it). You need at least three to play, and, fortunately, Dad and Andy know how, so that takes some of the pressure off me. Mom doesn't like to play with me, anyway. She says I just get rid of all my bad cards at the very first opportunity without any sense of what's happening in the game (which she's pretty much right about). I thought getting rid of the bad cards (hearts and the queen of spades) as soon as you could was the whole point. Basically I hate card games.

Dad's playing at the Oahu Country Club with one of the navy men who is related to Senator Mucky Muck. He got up real early because they have to "tee off" by 7:00 A.M.

Dad doesn't dress like golfers are supposed to dress. I watched out the window when Senator Mucky Muck's nephew (I think) came to pick Dad up.

He looked like he had spent hours in front of the mirror trying to decide how to assemble clothes that had the most amount of checks and plaids (he succeeded). But Dad just had on his old Harvard sweat suit (that's where he went to school) and a towel around his neck.

He already has a golf date for the next three Sunday mornings. We'll never get to see him anymore on Sundays.

Tomorrow, school.

This time, I'm going to take Mom's advice. I'm not going to have one best friend, even if someone begs me. I'm going to have two or three friends, maybe even more.

Mom's going to drive me in the new car. It's a brand-new four-door Hudson, and it has a foot-controlled radio-station selector that is really, really fun (although I have to scrunch down a little in the driver's seat so I can reach it).

Monday, November 10, 1941
Oahu, Hawaii

School wasn't as bad as I thought it would be. Of course I did have to go through the being-escorted-by-the-principal-and-being-introduced-to-the-entire-class routine.

Most of the kids look like me, but there are also Hawaiian, Japanese, Chinese, and lots of kids who look like they're all of these combined.

Everyone's pretty friendly. One girl stopped me in the hall and said that if I needed help going over any of the stuff I missed to just let her know. She's in most of my classes and has really, really white teeth and the nicest smile I've ever seen. Her name is Kame Arata.

I was surprised she spoke English so well. I never knew anyone Japanese (at least I think she's Japanese), and it's funny seeing someone like her who sounds pretty much just like me.

Wednesday, November 12, 1941
Oahu, Hawaii

It was Andy's birthday yesterday (he's sixteen, so he'll be even more obnoxious). Mom and Dad gave him binoculars, and Grandpa and Grandma sent him a silver dollar, which they always give us on our birthday.

Dad said he would take Andy up to Aiea

Heights with his binoculars so he could see all the way down to Pearl Harbor, which is where the boats are.

Andy wants to join the Boy Scouts. Mom asked if I wanted to become a Girl Scout, but I don't. Rules and regulations aren't my favorite things in the world. Most rules don't really make any sense — like looking both ways but what if it's a one-way street? Plus, I don't think I look so nice in a uniform.

Thursday, November 13, 1941
Oahu, Hawaii

Mom and Dad went out to a big-deal dinner on the Waikiki Terrace, which is up on the roof of the Royal Hawaiian Hotel. The reason I know it was a big deal is because Dad wore his white tuxedo jacket and Mom wore a gown.

Mom said the Royal Hawaiian Orchestra was going to play (from the way she said it, I think they're famous), and there was going to be lots of champagne, which Mom really likes.

Friday, November 14, 1941
Oahu, Hawaii

Dad's writing his first article since we got here. One of the Ten Commandments of the Billows family is THOU SHALT NOT INTERRUPT DAD WHEN HE'S WRITING AN ARTICLE. This is in effect no matter how urgent you think it is that you've lost your tooth. (I used to interrupt him quite a bit when I was younger).

I hardly ever interrupt him now, though. It's not that he yells or anything like that. Frankly, that would be better. He just looks up slowly from his precious Smith-Corona (another commandment: DON'T TOUCH THE SMITH-CORONA — "it's not a toy") and asks what you came to see him about. He's not really too glad to see you, but he thinks that being polite and getting to the point of your unannounced and unwanted visit is simply the fastest way to get rid of you.

I'd rather he just yelled, "GET OUT." Dad's the type who can kill you with kindness.

His articles always look nice and clean when he starts out. But by day two, he's scribbled all over the margins; by day three, he's crossed out some things, circled others, and drawn arrows showing where he now thinks some things should go. When it's impossible for anyone but him to decipher what he's written, it's ready to be read to Mom (he always changes anything that Mom says doesn't sound right). Then it's ready for its final retyping (Dad's a ferocious two-finger typist), which means he will be awash in a sea of crumpled-up white typing paper for the next twenty-four hours (at least) and won't eat or drink anything except coffee.

★★★

Monday, November 17, 1941
Oahu, Hawaii

This is the first time in my entire life that I have needed *anyone's* help with my schoolwork. Each time we move, though, it gets harder because I miss so much, and now that I'm in the sixth grade the work is *really* getting hard. (Last year was the first year I didn't get straight A's because of that stupid A– in science — thanks to Mr. Gould, better known as Mr. Ghoul.)

Science is where I'm having trouble. History, math, English, and social studies are fine. But what they're doing in science is *so* different that I really need some help.

Kame said that after school Wednesday we could walk home to her house together and then my mom could pick me up after dinner.

Mom said that means she's inviting me to stay for dinner and it would be rude to say no.

One of the class mothers called Mom and asked if she would like to join the PTA. Mom said we were still getting settled and just as soon as we were "unpacked" she would "check back." Mom says the same thing in every city we move to.

Tuesday, November 18, 1941
Oahu, Hawaii

Mom picked us up after school, as usual, but the surprise was that Dad and I were going to the Hawaiian Book Exchange (Mom was taking Andy to his first Boy Scout meeting).

Dad's finished with his article and he was celebrating. Dad celebrates almost everything by buying some more books. He's not comfortable when we move to a new city until he's found a "decent" secondhand bookstore. That's where he met Mom. Dad was working part-time in a secondhand bookstore while he was going to college. Mom came in wearing her nurse's uniform — that's what Mom was before Andy was born — and was standing on her tiptoes — she's pretty petite — trying to get a cookbook off a really, really high shelf. That's when Dad swooped in for the kill. He snatched the book down off the shelf, blew off some imaginary dust, and said, "Al Billows, at your service." (That's why I was named Amber, and Andy, Andy. Mom's first name is Anne, and since Dad's Al, everyone's initials had to be A. B.) Then he handed her the book with a flourish, and as they say, the rest is history.

Mr. Poole's Hawaiian Book Exchange is pretty dusty and dark, which is precisely what Dad means by "decent." It has to have at least a million books, and the more disorderly the better. It must have at least a million books just up in the balcony. I didn't go up there, though, because it looked to me like the whole thing was about to collapse.

Dad really hit it off with the man who owns the store. He had wild, gray hair that went all over the place and looked like it had *never, ever* been combed; wore glasses that hung by a string around his neck but which he never put on his face; and smoked a cigar that he never lit. But he sounded the opposite of the way he looked. He seemed so intelligent and had a soothing, soft voice that was as gentle as a whisper.

Just listening to him talk made you feel everything was going to be all right.

Usually Dad likes to have everyone else do all the talking, but this time Dad was. The bookstore man wanted to know what people "back on the mainland" thought about the war, especially the people back in Washington.

Mr. Poole asked me if I liked to read, and when I said very much, he seemed delighted. He said in that case he had a delightful surprise for me, and disappeared down one of the long, dimly lit aisles that separated the endless rows of floor-to-ceiling bookcases. When he returned, he handed me a copy of *The Secret Garden* and said he hoped I enjoyed it half as much as he did.

When Dad paid for his books, Mr. Poole wouldn't let him pay for mine, pointing to the sign over his head: CHILDREN READ FOR FREE.

Dad liked Mr. Poole so much, he asked me if it was all right if he joined us for dinner. It was fine with me — I didn't even know we were going to have dinner out.

When we left, the man just turned the OPEN/CLOSED sign the other way, and off we went. He suggested we take a streetcar to his favorite restaurant, which was a lot of fun. I had two orders of the best spareribs.

We were all having such a good time (when Dad genuinely likes someone, which is actually quite rare, he *really* likes them), Mr. Poole came with us to the movies.

Dad *loves* the movies, and so do I. (Mom would rather read, and Andy would rather play baseball.) And Dad *loves* Charlie Chaplin, so we went to see *The Great Dictator* at the Princess Theater.

Dad and I prefer to go to the movies in the afternoon, and so, it turns out, does Mr. Poole. Mr. Poole said that going to the movies in the afternoon is the best because there aren't enough people there to ruin it for you by talking. And, besides, he said, it's more fun going in the afternoon because "it's so wicked" — he winked at me when he said that.

Charlie Chaplin was really, really funny, especially when he was imitating Hitler. I don't understand, however, how everyone can laugh at someone who's supposed to be so awful.

Wednesday, November 19, 1941
Oahu, Hawaii

Kame's house is very pretty. There were two peacocks roaming around the gardens.

There are photographs and things all over the walls. In the living room there was a picture of someone who looked like he must be the king of

Japan, and two swords, one long and one short. Kame said that they were samurai swords, and that her ancestors had been samurai warriors back in Japan.

When we sat down to dinner I was surprised that there were no forks, only chopsticks. I didn't have the vaguest idea what to do with them. Everyone, including her two younger brothers, was looking at me like they were expecting me to do something miraculous, like actually eat with them.

Kame realized what my dilemma was and brought a fork and spoon from the drawer. Now that I had utensils I could use, it seemed to be a kind of signal that everyone could begin passing the food around.

There were steaming bowls of noodles, platters of rice cakes, little bowls of dried squid, tempura, and tofu, which I had never even heard of. The tofu was nicer than I thought, smooth and velvety, like custard but not nearly as tasty.

Kame explained that tofu was made from ground soya beans, hoping, I think, that that would mean something to me.

Mr. Arata asked me how I liked living in Hawaii, and I said that, although I had only been here a short time, it seemed quite nice. (I hate it when people say something is "quite nice.") He said that Hawaii was *tenjiku,* which means it is a "heavenly place." Mr. Arata owns a tea importing company.

After dinner he played the samisen, which is a three-stringed Japanese guitar, and everyone (except me, of course) sang Japanese songs. Even though I couldn't join in, I liked being there, because her family is very sweet.

When we were in Kame's room waiting for Mom to pick me up, she said that her mother didn't speak at dinner because, in a traditional Japanese family, the woman must always defer to the man.

She said the Japanese have a saying: "There is

no prosperity in a family where the hen crows." Which means that women are silent, and men rule the roost.

She sounded like she thought she owed me an explanation.

She asked me if my family was traditional or modern. I had never thought about that. The only thing I knew was that Dad sure didn't rule our roost, but I didn't know if that made us traditional or modern. The only thing I knew about our family is that we were real different from most families.

She said her family favored her brothers because Japanese parents only want boys for children.

She sounded very sad.

She told me her name means "turtle" in Japanese, and I couldn't help but laugh. It took me quite a while to stop while Kame was saying, "What? What? What's so funny?" I finally calmed down enough to tell her about Andy and the sharks and the surfers, and she started laughing again and said now she was never going in the ocean again, thanks to me.

Sunday, November 23, 1941
Oahu, Hawaii

Dad's already off to golf, so I stayed in bed later than usual and reread Allison's letter, which arrived yesterday.

She said that she already misses me just as much as she thought she would. She's sure by now I've already found a new best friend. She said she saw Sylvia Prescott once or twice, which was fine, but every time she would wear something Sylvia liked, Sylvia would go out the very next day and buy it (her father is rich) and then wear it to school.

She wants to know everything about Hawaii, especially what all the kids in school are like.

She said she misses me and misses being with my family, especially having ice cream after dinner. Allison loved to talk to Mom. She would tell Mom things she wouldn't even tell me (that's how I knew about her father being in the hospital). Mom's a great listener — something that most people (including me) aren't too good at. Mom said that's because people just like to hear the sound of their own voice.

Mom said that if I don't write Allison back this week, she's going to strangle me. She said she had no intention of raising an inconsiderate daughter, which I thought was unnecessary.

Monday, November 24, 1941
Oahu, Hawaii

Andy is having a heart attack because he discovered that one of his new friends (he already has about a thousand) has an even better baseball-card collection than he does. Andy basically judges people on the size and quality of their baseball-card collections (which partially explains why Andy doesn't know any girls — but only partially).

According to Andy, this one boy has a 1937 Joe DiMaggio, and the big news is that he's willing to trade it, but Andy says he wants too much in return. Andy's a pretty shrewd bargainer, especially when it comes to his baseball cards.

Mom and I went shopping for all the stuff we need for Thanksgiving dinner. It's going to be really strange having Thanksgiving dinner without, one, Grandma and Grandpa; and, two, snow. It's not even cold!

On the way there, Mom said she was hoping we could find a nice, fat pig so she could make stone-cooked pig for everyone. (Dad's invited Mr. Poole and Lieutenant Something, his golfing friend.)

Tuesday, November 25, 1941
Oahu, Hawaii

Kame's trying to convince me to join the Shakespeare Club. Now I'm sorry I told her how much I like acting and about all the stuff Allison and I did last year. They're going to do *Much Ado About Nothing,* which is one of my favorites, so it's tempting.

I still feel too new here and not comfortable enough to be in a play yet. To be in a play you have to really, really feel comfortable with the other people, and I don't even know anyone besides Kame.

She said they will be holding auditions over the next two weeks, so I don't have to decide right now, which let me off the hook. I can tell, though, that Kame is going to be disappointed if I don't do it.

At least she's happy I promised I would go to the big dance with her on Sunday, December 7. It's in the big hall at school, and Mom said she would drive us, pick us up, and take Kame home.

Sunday night we went skating at the Waikiki Skating Arena, which was a lot of fun. We skated with some boys Kame knows. Kame is really, really pretty, so she know lots of boys.

Kame likes to do all sorts of stuff, which is good. She's never boring, which is my greatest fear in life. If someone asked me what would be my least favorite way to die, I would say being bored to death.

I'm trying really hard not to have a best friend. But it seems to be happening without my doing anything. It's not my fault because Kame is just like me, and she's popular and pretty so it's not like she was lonely until I came around. It's just that she likes to be with me the most, and I feel the same.

She's staying with her aunt, Miss Kozuke, for two nights. Kame loves her aunt, who is much younger than her mother and more modern. Kame says her aunt believes you take what is best from the land of your ancestors and the land of your birth. One is not necessarily better than the other.

Her aunt is the reason Kame speaks English as well as she does. Her aunt believes it is very important to speak English properly. When Kame stays at her house, they don't speak any Japanese and they read the newspaper aloud so that Kame can keep practicing. Kame said that if her mother found out, she would be very angry.

I asked Kame if she was worried that America and Japan might soon be at war with each other. (This is what Daddy wrote about in his article. He titled it "Collision Course.")

She said she would be very sad because if that happened, she knows it would trouble her mother and father terribly because they were born in Japan. But she was born right here in Honolulu, and she's American, not Japanese.

She just hopes it doesn't happen.

Thursday, November 27, 1941
Oahu, Hawaii

You could tell that Thanksgiving this year was not going to be like previous years from the moment the guests arrived. Lieutenant Lockhart came in a chauffeur-driven car with flags flying from the fenders, and Mr. Poole by bike wearing tennis shoes and his yellow rain slicker, although there wasn't a cloud in the sky.

I think it would have been better if there were wives, but Mr. Poole isn't married, and Lieutenant Lockhart's wife is back home in Pasadena, California.

I'm not sure if Dad thought Mr. Poole and Lieutenant Lockhart would get along or if he thought about it at all and it was just that neither of them had anyplace special to be on Thanksgiving. You can never tell with Dad: It's very hard to read his mind.

Whatever he was thinking, it was not one of

his better ideas. As Mom likes to say, "The tension was so thick, you could cut it with a knife."

The only thing they agreed on was how good Mom's turkey was. (Of course, I'm the only one who knew how close they came to having a nice, fat, juicy pig instead of a turkey for Thanksgiving dinner.)

Early on, Dad tried to loosen things up by telling a lame joke. Dad thinks he's a great joke teller, but he isn't — neither in his choice or delivery. He said that, as everyone knew, some of the Hawaiian street names were very hard to pronounce. One day a new policeman, who had just come from the mainland, found a dead horse on Halekauwila Street, and rather than call it in he found someone to help him move the horse to King Street and then he called it in.

Ha. Ha.

Usually dinner party conversation starts out nice and relaxed, like everyone's just passing the time, with nothing particular on their minds, even though everyone knows that isn't the case. This time it didn't start off like that at all.

Once Lieutenant Lockhart got started, there was no stopping him. The only time he paused was when he asked to have his drink "freshened," which was something I thought only Mrs. Mouse said.

Mr. Poole was pretty quiet, and Dad hardly said a word, which was a sure sign he was delighted with the conversation and had already started mentally writing his next article. Even Mom, who usually joins in quite readily, was on the quiet side. But you could tell she was listening intently to every word.

Right before dessert, Mr. Poole got this funny look in his eye, like he'd just had an inspiration. He asked Lieutenant Lockhart if he was aware that war with Japan was "just around the corner," and it was just a question of where and when.

Lieutenant Lockhart laughed, like he had heard

the best joke ever. He started to lecture Mr. Poole as if he were talking to someone whose intelligence he considered way below his.

Japan, he explained, was a second-rate country with a third-rate military. Their aviators had such poor vision, they couldn't even fly their airplanes properly — their air force had the highest accident rate in the world.

Lieutenant Lockhart's voice was getting louder with each sentence, as if the size of his audience were growing and he wanted to make sure he was being heard, even in the back rows. He sounded like someone who was used to having the final word on any subject.

Japan wouldn't dare face the United States in battle, he went on. It was inconceivable that the Japanese government was unaware of these facts and the risks involved and would refrain, he was sure, from doing anything foolhardy.

The only sign that Mr. Poole was thinking anything at all was a slight downturn at the corners of his mouth, and a lowering of his eyelids, like he was growing tired of the conversation.

Sometimes Mr. Poole talks in riddles, and it's not quite clear precisely what he's saying, although you usually have an idea of what he's getting at. Dad says Mr. Poole's a poet and a "true scholar."

He picked up his unlit cigar and looked at it for a moment and then said to Lieutenant Lockhart: "Experience is a costly school, Lieutenant. But a fool will learn in no other."

He said it in his usual, friendly, off-the-cuff way, like he was simply notifying you that it might rain tomorrow and perhaps you should take an umbrella.

By now, Lieutenant Lockhart was visibly agitated and didn't even respond when Mom asked him if he would like another piece of pecan pie. Instead, he downed his drink and signaled to Dad that he was ready for another.

When he spoke, he was angry and his pupils had become tiny black pellets.

The Japanese in Japan didn't worry him one bit, he said. It was the Japanese living right here in Hawaii who worried him. Only he didn't say "Japanese." He said "Buddha-heads." He said, "Almost half the goddamn population of Hawaii is 'Buddha-heads,'" and he wouldn't be surprised if they begin sabotage operations any day now.

He bragged that the entire Pearl Harbor military base was on full alert, twenty-four hours a day, to guard against any sabotage attempts that "these Buddha-heads think they can make."

He suggested that Mr. Poole stick his nose back in his books and not where it doesn't belong. He said he should leave military strategy to military strategists like himself.

That's when Mr. Poole got up.

He shuffled over to where Lieutenant Lockhart was sitting and stood behind him so that Lieutenant Lockhart would have to turn around in his chair if he wanted to face him.

Mr. Poole asked him, still in his soft, gentle

voice, how long he had lived in Hawaii. Two months, Lieutenant Lockhart replied, quickly, without moving.

Mr. Poole said he had lived in Hawaii fifty-four years, all his life. He said that he was fortunate to have gotten to know many, many Japanese during that time. He said he could assure the lieutenant that, although Japan was their home-land, America was their chosen land, and we had nothing to fear from them.

He leaned over, as if what he had to say was private, between Lieutenant Lockhart and him-self. He was almost whispering. "The Japanese have an ancient proverb, Lieutenant Lockhart," he said. "Roughly translated it is as follows: Be-hold the frog, who when he opens his mouth, displays his whole inside."

Then he thanked Mom for "a glorious repast," told Dad he hoped to see him at the bookstore soon, winked at me and Andy, and said he would see himself to the door.

Sunday, November 30, 1941
Oahu, Hawaii

After Thanksgiving dinner I wasn't at all sure we were going on the tour of Pearl Harbor that Lieutenant Lockhart had offered to take us on. I'm not sure what Dad would have done if it were up to him, but he knew that Andy would be really disappointed if we didn't go. So the three of us went. Not Mom, though. She wouldn't budge. She told Dad that she had seen and heard enough of Lieutenant Lockhart to last her a lifetime. This must be what Dad means when he says Mom doesn't suffer fools gladly.

I hadn't seen Andy this excited since the Dodgers won the pennant. He asked Lieutenant Lockhart so many questions, he could hardly catch his breath. He was talking so fast, I was afraid he was going to have an asthma attack right then and there.

We all went over to Hickham Field, where the American bombers are, and to Wheeler, where the fighters are based. The fighter planes were lined up neatly on the ground, wing to wing and close together so they could more readily be protected from sabotage, Lieutenant Lockhart explained.

I had to hand it to Andy: He knew what each plane was, how fast it could go, everything. Lieutenant Lockhart said he was quite impressed, and you could see that he was.

We saw battleship row, and got to see the cruisers, destroyers, and the battleships. We were lucky, because all the battleships were there for the first time in months.

But Andy was disappointed because the aircraft carriers (his favorites) were out on maneuvers and weren't there.

The last thing we did was take a tour of Lieutenant Lockhart's own ship, the U.S.S. *Arizona*. We watched a boxing match that was held onboard. The ship was most impressive. It was so clean, it gleamed in the sun, and the crew wore their white dress uniforms and saluted us as we passed.

Monday, December 1, 1941
Oahu, Hawaii

I got another letter from Allison. Amazingly enough, they're doing *Much Ado About Nothing* also. I think I'll join the Shakespeare Club with Kame and be in the play. Then Allison and I can be doing the same play at the same time. Maybe even the same role!

Mom said this was my last warning: If I don't write back to Allison by the end of the week, it's "curtains."

Mom said as far as she's concerned, life is easier here. Just not wearing so many clothes all the time is a relief.

Mom asked me how I liked school and if I was

making lots of friends. I think she was hinting at our best-friend discussion, but I know she likes Kame so she didn't say anything else about it.

Kame and I have to decide by Thursday what we're going to wear to the dance Sunday night.

Tuesday, December 2, 1941
Oahu, Hawaii

While I was helping Mom prepare everything for dinner, I asked her if she liked living in Hawaii and if she missed the United States.

She said she was glad we were living here, because she thinks Dad is taking things a little easier. (Frankly, I hadn't noticed this. He seems to be working just as hard here as he did in Washington or Boston. Although there aren't nearly as many dinner parties, and maybe that's what Mom means. In Washington, there was one practically every weekend.)

Friday, December 5, 1941
Oahu, Hawaii

Dad's playing golf with another reporter. He's a friend of Mr. Poole and writes for the *Honolulu Advertiser*. Lieutenant Lockhart can't play this Sunday because he's on duty.

Saturday, December 6, 1941
Oahu, Hawaii

Mom and I went shopping. She needed new shoes, and so did I. After shopping we saw *Dark Victory*. Mom doesn't like to go to the movies as much as Dad and I do, but she does if it's a Bette Davis movie. It was a pretty gloomy story, if you ask me, but Mom likes gloomy stories.

✪✪✪

Sunday, December 7, 1941
Oahu, Hawaii

This is the third time I have attempted to write, but my hands have been shaking so badly that my writing is illegible. It seems steady enough now, and I will try to record all the horrible events that have taken place in the past twelve hours.

At first I thought I was still dreaming. I heard an incessant droning, like the sound the *China Clipper*'s propellers made, only much louder, more high-pitched.

Oddly, my mother was in the dream. She was saying, "Amber, Amber, wake up, wake up," her voice barely audible above the whining sound that was getting louder and closer. I could tell by the force of her voice that she was speaking as loudly as she could.

The dream was disturbing, but I didn't want to wake up because I was too sleepy. But now Mom was shaking me. I would have to get up.

The dream was over, and the nightmare was about to begin.

"Go wake your brother right now," she said.

I have never heard fear or panic in my mother's voice before, but I heard it then. There was no mistaking it.

I hadn't noticed that the droning in the dream was still there.

Without questioning what was so urgent or why I should get Andy up, I barged right into his room and told him Mom wanted him to get up right away.

I think some of the fear in Mom's voice must have been transmitted to mine, because Andy didn't question me any more than I questioned Mom.

We both ran downstairs, out the kitchen door, and onto the back patio, where Mom was, looking up at the sky.

She told Andy to go back and get his binoculars.

There were hundreds of planes in the sky. That's where the droning was coming from.

In the past few weeks I had gotten used to the sound of planes flying over my head while the army was on maneuvers. But this sound was different — it was louder, deeper, and there were more planes than I'd ever seen before. And, besides, the army never had maneuvers at eight o'clock on a Sunday morning.

They were coming in unbelievably low, barely clearing the treetops, circling in the sky and then peeling off, forming smaller groups of four and five.

Andy scanned the skies with his binoculars. He knew all the planes by heart: torpedo planes, high-level fliers, dive-bombers, horizontal bombers. Something was wrong, he said. They weren't the same color as our planes, and the red-ball insignias on the wings weren't American.

I was astonished when I looked through the binoculars. The planes were flying low enough that you could see them plainly even without the binoculars. But with them I could see right into the glass-paneled canopy that covered the cockpit where the pilot sat. I was going to wave like I had done so many times before, but I stopped.

The pilot had a white cloth tied around his forehead, and he looked just like Mr. Arata. He was Japanese! These were Japanese planes, not American planes on maneuvers. The pilot was smiling at me, looking close enough that I could reach out and touch him. Then he banked into a turn and was gone.

"It's Pearl Harbor! It's Pearl Harbor!" Andy was screaming. He was pointing to the column of black smoke that was rising up in the skies above Pearl Harbor. The smoke was mixing with the rays of the early morning sun, creating an eerie, bloodred sky.

There was machine-gun fire in the distance that sounded like Fourth of July firecrackers, and dull, booming explosions that were so loud, you could feel the ground shaking beneath your feet and hear the dishes rattling in the kitchen cabinets.

Mom had the radio on as loud as it would go. For a while there was no news, only a church service and some music.

I was praying Dad would call. I so wanted to hear his voice and know that he was all right.

Finally the announcer interrupted the program. "This is the real McCoy," he said. "We are under attack. The Japs are here." He kept repeating it and repeating it, like he was trying to convince himself it just wasn't another drill.

Andy was right. They were attacking Pearl Harbor.

But that was all we knew. We didn't know if anyone had been killed or hurt or even if there was anyone left at Pearl Harbor.

Outside, there were more explosions, different from the ones earlier. Andy said they were anti-aircraft guns.

Directly over our heads we saw the first American plane. He was going after a Japanese fighter. They were desperately trying to outmaneuver each other. We watched the struggle transfixed and horrified.

Finally the American plane's stream of bullets found their target.

The Japanese plane exploded with such violence that in a moment it ceased to be a plane. It was a flaming, orange inferno hurtling toward the earth.

There were more announcements and more instructions on the radio: Don't drive, stay off the streets, don't use telephones, prepare buckets of sand, and fill tubs with water in case of fire.

The announcer sounded frantic, his voice faltering.

He said all doctors and nurses who were in the area should come immediately to the army's Tripler General Hospital.

When Mom said she had to go, I looked at her

in utter disbelief. It was another incredible shock on top of the ones I was still trying to absorb. I couldn't understand how she could even consider leaving us here. We hadn't heard from Dad — we didn't know where he was, or even if he was all right.

My whole world was disintegrating right before my eyes, like that Japanese plane that had been shot down only minutes ago.

Mom looked at me like she was depending on me for something. *I have to do this, please help me,* her look said.

I said nothing, and that was sufficient.

She told us not to leave the house, no matter what. That we should stay away from windows and doors and wait until Dad got home and tell him where she went and not to worry. If anything happened, we should lock ourselves in the basement. This was an insight into the state of Mom's mind. We don't have a basement.

Then she hugged us, got in the car, and drove off.

I decided I would be safer if I was hiding under something. Andy helped me turn over the couch and the two big chairs, push them together in the middle of the living room, and drape our blankets and sheets over them.

It took a lot of time and it was hard to move everything around, but it was worth it. I decided I needed one last thing. I went to the kitchen and got Mom's big cleaver. Once I was back inside the couch-fort I felt safer, although I could only stay for fifteen minutes at a time because I could hardly breathe.

A little after we built the couch-fort, Dad called.

He was all right and wanted to know if we were all right. Andy told him we were, and then I spoke to him. I told him Mom had gone to help out at the hospital, and he didn't say anything for the longest time. Then he said he would go there first, get Mom, and come home.

Like Mom, he wanted me to tell him that it was okay, so I did, although I wish Mom hadn't gone to the hospital, or Dad to play golf, and that he would just come home and that we had never left Washington in the first place.

I was too terrified to do anything besides listen to reports on the radio. They kept repeating the same instructions as before and urging everyone to be calm.

Andy, despite instructions, stayed outside till it was dark, looking up at the skies with his binoculars, tears streaming down his face. I don't know what he was looking at. There was nothing to see. There had been no planes, no explosions since Mom had left.

I remained inside under the couch until Mom and Dad came home.

★★★

Monday, December 8, 1941
Oahu, Hawaii

Andy and I slept in our sleeping bags on the floor in Mom and Dad's room (although I don't think any of us got much sleep).

I don't know what I would have done if they hadn't come home or if anything had happened to them. I feel much better now that we're all together.

Mom made breakfast like there was nothing unusual happening. Andy and I just sat there at the kitchen table, waiting for Dad to say something.

He said when they had seen where the planes were headed, they'd driven to Pearl Harbor. The skies overhead were already turning gray from the black smoke spewing up from the badly damaged ships along battleship row.

It looked like the entire fleet had been destroyed. All of Pearl Harbor was in flames, and the harbor itself was a lake of fire. The beach was littered with the limp bodies of the men who had been washed ashore.

Everyone was running all over the place. It was the first time many of the men had seen any real action. When Dad said this, he put his head in his hands for a few seconds. I looked quickly at Mom and could see she was trying not to cry.

Some of the men became unglued, others panicked, and still others were frozen with fear. Some of the men were badly burned from swimming in the scalding water trying to save themselves and their buddies. Others, heroically, refused to abandon their antiaircraft guns, ignoring the flames that were about to engulf them. Many risked their lives going belowdecks to help their trapped crewmates.

Hundreds had been killed, maybe more.

Worst hit were the *Oklahoma* and the *Arizona,* Lieutenant Lockhart's ship.

The *Oklahoma* took five torpedoes, and most of the men were trapped and drowned when the ship capsized. Some are still alive in a compartment at the bottom of the ship that is now the top of the ship.

They can hear them tapping, but it's nearly impossible to tell precisely where the tapping is coming from because the sound echoes throughout the vessel. The rescue workers had been using acetylene torches to cut through the ship's hull, but the flame used up all the oxygen and suffocated some of the men to death. They switched to safer cutting equipment, but that is taking longer and they know that every second, the water inside is rising.

The men from the Navy Yard plan to work all night long.

The *Arizona* was hit the worst. At least eight bombs landed, and one went straight down one of the ship's funnels. It landed in the part of the ship where all the ammunition was stored, and there was a horrendous chain reaction that ignited cans of black powder, thousands of rounds of machine-gun bullets, and all the torpedoes. The whole front part of the *Arizona* exploded, and fire raged all over the ship.

Dad said he didn't see how anyone could have survived.

Nearly all the planes at Hickham and Wheeler have been destroyed also. Some Japanese pilots who had been shot down aimed their mortally wounded planes at hangars and rows of parked planes in one last suicide attack.

We all remained silent while Dad spoke. When he was done, we looked at Mom. But Mom obviously didn't want to talk about last night at the hospital. When she came home she looked dazed, and her pretty yellow dress was splattered with dried blood. All she said was that she wanted to lie down for a while.

"I have to go back," she said, staring down into her coffee cup.

But this time I was ready for her.

I told her I was going with her.

I had thought about it all last night. I wasn't going to spend another day hiding under the couch, wondering where everyone was, if they would ever come back, and hoping that the Japanese planes didn't drop a bomb on my head.

I was going, and there was nothing she or Dad could do to stop me.

I knew my face had to show how determined I was. Any signs of second thoughts, doubts, or any weakness whatsoever and Mom was sure to make me stay behind.

I showed none.

She looked at Dad wordlessly.

Dad said Andy could go with him, to Honolulu.

As we drove to the hospital we could see that the destruction had not been confined to Pearl Harbor.

There were houses wrecked by bombs, stores that were smoldering ruins, and bomb craters so deep, a man could stand in them.

There were roadblocks everywhere. The MPs,

carrying rifles with long bayonets, stopped our car, looked inside, and asked Mom what her destination was. When Mom told one she was a nurse and she was going to Tripler, he immediately waved us through.

It still took three times longer than it usually did. There were traffic jams wherever we turned. Accidents littered the road and the roadsides, making for slow going.

As soon as we arrived, there were a thousand things to do.

There were hundreds of men lined up in the halls, still lying on the stretchers that they had been brought in on by the litter bearers and the ambulance teams. Emergency ambulances continued to drive up depositing more badly wounded men, including some of the men who had finally been freed from the *Oklahoma*.

Patients who had been hospitalized before the Japanese attack willingly gave up their beds. Still, some of the stretchers had to remain outside on the grass until there was space available in the constantly overcrowded halls.

The stench was overpowering. Some of the men were burned so badly, their flesh had turned black. It's a smell I don't think I will ever forget.

A medical officer walked up and down the halls deciding who was fortunate enough to be treated next. Doctors and nurses worked furiously at the operating tables while orderlies, frantic that they were running out of sterilized instruments, sutures, and bandages, searched for the necessary equipment while seeing to the patients waiting their turn.

It is a miracle they were able to concentrate on the grim tasks before them.

Everything and everyone was moving so fast, it was a blur, with barely enough time to react and realize how truly horrible it all was.

Mom told me I should help organize the people who were lined up to donate blood. She told me to work fast because some men were going into shock since they were losing so much blood. There were so many people in line that they had run out of proper containers, and we had to use sterilized Coke bottles.

Many of the people in line were Japanese, which surprised me. I know it shouldn't have, but it did. It was the first time since early Sunday morning that I had thought about Kame, if she was all right, if her family was safe, and how awful this must be for her.

One man was so nervous about giving blood, I told him that maybe he shouldn't. He insisted, saying he wanted to do his part. But when I asked him to roll up his sleeve, he fainted.

After that, I cleaned all the dirty bottles and tubes I could find, gathered containers that were scattered all over, washed them, and filled them with water so Mom could sterilize the instruments.

When I started to take off the soiled sheets from one recently vacated bed, thinking I would put on fresh, clean ones, Mom stopped me. We had no time for that. The next patient would just have to be put in the bed as it was.

These poor boys bore their excruciating pain in stony silence, most moaning quietly to themselves, as if they didn't want to cause any trouble or disturb anyone.

One patient was in shock from loss of blood. Mom said I should just do my best to comfort him. I put my hand under his head, lifted it up, and gave him a drink of water. He smiled, as if to say thanks.

He was trying so hard to talk, desperately wanting to tell me something that seemed terribly important to him. But no matter how hard he tried, he couldn't utter a sound. I summoned all my acting ability so he would think that I understood, and, in a way, I think I did.

When I returned a few minutes later to check on him, he didn't look too good. I found Mom. She felt for a pulse and put her ear to his mouth to see if he was breathing. There was nothing. With no emotion showing on her face, Mom pulled the sheet over his head and, in a matter-of-fact voice, said that I should see to the other patients.

There was one man who had been screaming the same thing over and over for hours.

"Where are they? Where are they?" he kept shouting. It seemed that no one dared approach him, and I felt bad for him. I wanted to do something, although, God knows, I didn't know what.

I held his hand, which was cold as ice and soaked with sweat. He stopped screaming, at least for the moment. I brought a basin of cool water with me and I dipped a ragged piece of cloth into the water, then gently laid it on his brow, which seemed to be burning up with fever.

He was lying there with his eyes wide open, wild with fear and distorted with pain.

He looked familiar, but I couldn't remember where I knew him from. Then, I realized who he was.

It was Lieutenant Lockhart.

He started screaming again, as if my recognition had caused him to cry out. I hurried to find Mom.

I think at first she didn't believe me. It had already been a hideously long and awful day. I think she thought I was delirious. I didn't blame her for thinking that, but I wasn't.

When she looked down at Lieutenant Lockhart, her expression was difficult to decipher. It was disdainful and sympathetic at the same time.

She told me not to leave his side and returned within seconds with a syringe, which she immediately poked into his arm. In moments he was sleeping soundly.

On the way home, Mom told me she discovered that Lieutenant Lockhart had been thrown clear of the *Arizona* when the explosions first began. Although both his legs were severely injured, he was able to swim to shore where he collapsed. He was rescued and taken to the hospital, where they had to amputate both his legs in order to save his life.

Saturday, December 13, 1941
Oahu, Hawaii

This is the first night I've been able to write. For the past three nights I've just been too tired. As soon as Mom and I get home from the hospital, I stick something in my mouth, crawl into my sleeping bag, and I'm out like a light.

I feel a little rested now, and tomorrow we're not going to the hospital, which is quite a relief.

We're now under martial law, which means that the military has taken over the government. Mom said that she doesn't see why anyone would want the military taking over after the fine job they did of preventing the attack in the first place. I don't think Mom and Dad quite see eye to eye on this point, so the less I say, the better.

There are all sorts of stories going around about the attack. The Japanese on the island cut arrows in the cane fields pointing toward Pearl Harbor to guide the pilots; some of the pilots who were shot down have turned out to be graduates of high schools right here on Oahu! One of them was even wearing a McKinley High School class ring!

Andy and Dad went to look at one of the Japanese planes that was shot down. Andy said they had all the pilot's clothes laid out. He had American money, and he didn't wear a uniform. He wore American slacks and a typical, colorful sport shirt. All this so no one could tell where he came from if he survived the crash.

Andy has been going out with some of his friends and looking for souvenirs. So far they have found a half-burned Japanese flag, some bullets, and a wing section with the Rising Sun insignia on it. They're going to make key chains out of the bullets and sell them.

Andy and his friends want to go see the Japanese prisoner they captured from the midget submarine. According to my brother, these midget subs were launched on the backs of the regular-sized, mother subs and had only one or two men in them. One was rammed and sunk, and the man who was driving was captured.

And there are rumors that it's not over: The Japanese are coming back to destroy any ships and planes that survived the first attack; they're going to launch a ground invasion and take over all Hawaii; they've poisoned our reservoirs, and it isn't safe to drink the water; the Japanese on the island are going to rise up and kill all the *haoles* ("white people") on the island. And there's even a rumor that the United States has surrendered.

Dad says this is preposterous. The United States has declared war on Japan. He read President Roosevelt's speech to us. The president called December 7 "a date which will live in infamy," and said the attack was "unprovoked and dastardly."

People are trigger-happy, shooting at anything that moves. Last night a poor cow that got loose and was roaming around got shot.

People are rushing to the markets and grabbing anything they can off the shelves and putting it in their baskets without even looking at what it is.

Mom and I went shopping on the way home from the hospital, and it was awful. We had to wait an hour before we could even get into the Kaimuki Supermarket. They were told not to sell to people who were hoarding, just to sell the regular amount. But it was nearly impossible to control everyone. People were cradling ten-pound bags of rice, carrying cartons of canned milk and toilet paper out to their cars.

They finally had to close the doors and let in only a few people at a time.

Mom was a little worried because she wants to eat right because of the baby. She's getting a little big now, and you can feel the baby kick.

Mom's due in May. Maybe the baby will be born on my birthday, May 9!

Sunday, December 14, 1941
Oahu, Hawaii

Dad and Andy are almost finished making sure the kitchen and the bedroom are completely blackout proof.

For the past week (I can't believe it's only been a week — it seems like ten lifetimes) we have had sheets covering the windows, but that isn't working well enough.

Thursday night the air-raid warden came to our door and told us light was escaping from the kitchen window. (There can't be any light visible from sundown to sunup, and civilians are not allowed on the streets during that time.) The blackout is so no one accidentally or on purpose can give signals to the Japanese, should they return.

Mom thinks the blackout is pretty silly because Pearl Harbor is lit up all night long while the vessels are repaired. Dad said the military claims they can turn the lights off immediately if they need to. Mom wasn't exactly buying that.

Andy went around and stuffed cracks with newspapers. Now he and Dad are painting all the windows in both rooms black so that absolutely no light can escape.

Sometimes it gets too stuffy at night with the windows closed, so we open one. (We all sleep in Mom and Dad's room — Andy dragged in his mattress, but I still use my sleeping bag.) I can't go to sleep without reading at least a little while. So, to be on the safe side, I get into my sleeping bag before I turn on my flashlight.

We spend most of our time now either in the kitchen or the bedroom because they're the only two rooms that are blacked out.

Tuesday, December 16, 1941
Oahu, Hawaii

Mom asked if I wanted to go see Kame. I did and I didn't. Of course Mom sensed immediately what was going through my mind. In her let's-get-to-the-point tone of voice she said, "It's not Kame's fault."

We've decided to go see her tomorrow.

There hasn't been any school since December 7. The military has taken over our school buildings and turned them into administration offices and a processing center.

The military needs not only the buildings but our teachers, too. They are going door-to-door helping get all residents over the age of six finger-printed so they can be issued I.D. cards.

We'll have to carry the I.D. cards at all times. Andy said that one of the reasons is so our dead bodies can be easily identified in case of an attack. That took a big load off my mind.

School might not resume until February,

which is fine with me. I love spending time with the whole family, especially helping Mom with all the things we have to do.

Wednesday, December 17, 1941
Oahu, Hawaii

I was nervous all the way over to the Aratas', but as soon as I saw Kame's pretty face I knew in my heart how much I had missed her. I gave her a big hug, and I could feel how scared she was and could see it in her face.

Kame made tea, and we sat in the kitchen while she told us what had happened.

The Sunday night of the attack some MPs and a man from the FBI came to talk to her father.

They asked if he had a radio, and when he showed it to them they took it out to the car saying that they wanted to look it over at the lab.

One of the MPs took down the photograph and the samurai swords on the living–room wall and carted those out to the car also. Kame had told her father that morning to bury them, but he wouldn't listen to her.

After that her father, accompanied by the FBI man, went up to the bedroom. When he came down he was carrying a small suitcase. Mr. Arata said he was going downtown with the men to answer some of their questions and he would be back soon.

As her father was going out the door he turned to Kame and motioned for her to come close to him. He hugged her and told her, "You are the strong one. Take care of your mother and your brothers."

Then the man from the FBI put handcuffs on her father, put him in the car, and they drove away.

They haven't seen or heard from him since.

Kame tearfully told us that she and her mother are arguing over everything. Her mother yells at her for leaving a window open a crack, because she's deathly afraid one of the air-raid wardens will see some light and take her away, too. She said she has tried to obey her father's wishes but that she and her mother barely speak. (The whole time we were there, Mrs. Arata was upstairs with the two boys.)

One night her mother was on the telephone talking to Kame's aunt, and the operator came on the line and said something that her mother didn't understand. Kame's aunt explained, in Japanese, that the operator didn't want them to speak Japanese and that if they didn't start speaking English, they would have to get off the line.

Her mother hung up and started crying because she doesn't speak English well enough to do that.

All she ever says is *shikata ga nai,* which means "it can't be helped."

Kame is ashamed. Ashamed that she is Japanese. Ashamed that she has the face of the enemy. She is worried about her father. There are rumors that some of the men who have been rounded up by the authorities have been shot trying to escape. And she is worried about what will happen to her. She said she is afraid to go anywhere.

Mom said that she should remember that she is an American just like us, not the enemy. She told Kame she would have to give it time. Mom's a great believer in giving things time. Time is a healer, Mom likes to say.

Mom told Kame she would talk to Dad and see what he could find out about her father.

Then we invited Kame and her family (including her aunt) to Christmas dinner. Mom is determined to have Christmas dinner no matter how hard it is getting food.

You could see how pleased Kame was with the invitation — she even smiled a little. She said her aunt was an excellent cook and would prepare some delicious Japanese delicacies.

When we got home, we talked to Dad. He said the situation is grave because there is a great deal of hatred directed at the Japanese on the island. He said there is no telling what has happened to Mr. Arata, but he will do his best to find out where they have taken him.

Dad said he and Andy spent the whole day at his office trying to place calls to the mainland. He was able to speak to his paper's headquarters in New York City; to Grandma and Grandpa (who were relieved to hear his voice); and to the principal of our school in Washington. Dad wanted to let everyone know that we are all okay. That's the kind of thing Dad does all the time that makes him so sweet.

They got a late start coming home from Dad's office and had to drive the last two miles in the dark. Dad said it was really hard driving at night because the roads are so dark (there are no streetlights), and the headlights don't emit much light at all.

Last Thursday, Dad and Andy took the car down to the police station to have the headlights painted blue. Andy was pretty annoyed because they got blue paint all over the front of the car and, as with everything these days, they had to wait in line for over two hours.

Fortunately the car has running boards, so Andy stood on them and told Dad when he was getting too close to the side of the road.

Thursday, December 18, 1941
Oahu, Hawaii

Andy and Dad have been working nonstop for the past two days building our bomb shelter. It's supposed to be at least ten feet long and five feet wide, but ours doesn't look that big.

Dad got some corrugated iron that he's using for the roof. All they have to do is pile the dirt on the top and finish filling the sandbags for the back wall.

Mom said that from what she can see, it would be best if we were hit by a very, very small bomb.

Friday, December 19, 1941
Oahu, Hawaii

We had to stand in line for two hours today at the library waiting to get our gas masks. The man showed us how to put them on.

You have to place your chin in the mask first, then strap it over your head. There's this big, tubular part that comes down from your nose and mouth, so you look like an elephant with a mutated trunk.

I think there's as good a chance of suffocating to death from putting the gas mask on wrong as there is dying from a Japanese poison-gas attack.

You have to make sure it's on real, real tight so that no gas can get in. I feel like there's a squid attacking my face.

You're supposed to carry it in this ugly, green canvas bag with a shoulder strap. You have to take it with you *everywhere* — even to the bathroom. If the soldiers see you don't have it, they will make you go home and get it. And if you lose it, you have to pay $3.75 to get a new one.

The regular masks are too big for really little children and babies. They get "bunny bags," which their whole bodies go into, and there's a clear plastic area where their faces are. The bag has bunny ears, so they look like bunnies from outer space. It's pretty funny.

We went into a room to test and see if they actually worked. We put on our masks, and then they put tear gas in the room. My eyes got red and teary and felt real sore, so I raised my hand (which is what they told us to do if you were experiencing some gas), and they took me out immediately.

The man said my mask didn't fit right, which I had pretty much figured out by then.

Dad said the reason my mask doesn't fit is that my head is too small and that perhaps we should consider having it enlarged. Dad doesn't have the best sense of humor in the world. He said I shouldn't worry, because it's unlikely that any-thing is going to happen.

If it's unlikely that anything is going to happen, why do I have to wear it? (I didn't ask him that, because he has enough on his mind.)

Saturday, December 20, 1941
Oahu, Hawaii

I thought things couldn't get any worse, but I was wrong.

Mr. Poole is dead.

Dad and Andy went to see him at the bookstore. There was no bookstore. One of the American antiaircraft shells accidentally struck the build-ing when it missed its target and set it on fire. It burned to the ground.

Mr. Poole lived in an apartment in the same building as his store, and he died in the fire.

The whole block is still roped off.

Mom told me all this. Dad is still in the

bedroom. He hasn't come out since late this morning, when he and Andy got back. Andy said he's never seen Dad this upset about anything.

Sunday, December 21, 1941
Oahu, Hawaii

Dad's found out where Mr. Arata is. Since he was active in the Japanese Businessman's Association, he is suspected of somehow being involved in the December 7 attack. He's being held on Sand Island for questioning. That's all Dad knows.

Kame is relieved to know that her father is alive.

Monday, December 22, 1941
Oahu, Hawaii

Every time there's an air raid we rush out and cram ourselves into the bomb shelter. (Everyone except for Mom, that is. She said she would "rather be blown to smithereens than spend time in that crazy cave.")

Dad said people are building bigger and more elaborate ones. All we have in ours is a kerosene lantern, some canned food, but no can opener, and some bottled water.

It has two benches on either side when you walk in (or, more accurately, crawl in), a crude wooden floor, and a pipe going up through the roof so you can breathe, sort of.

There's always water seeping up from the ground, and there are mosquitoes, spiderwebs, snakes (I'm sure), and all sorts of horrible creatures with at least a thousand legs creeping and crawling around.

I wanted to ask Dad when he was going to put in the shower and bath, but I didn't dare. Dad hasn't been exactly ecstatic about his new building career. He works on his articles late at night in the kitchen because he spends so much time during the day on stuff like the bomb shelter.

Mom made a sign and put it over the entrance. It says: BILLOWS FAMILY — PLEASE KNOCK.

In the beginning I was always the first one down there because I was so scared. But now I don't rush down so fast, which is what I think Dad and Andy are doing, because no matter how slow I am, I'm still the first.

Tuesday, December 23, 1941
Oahu, Hawaii

This is going to be, without doubt, the worst Christmas of my life.

For one thing, there's downtown. They've painted all the buildings so that they're camouflaged. That way, they can't be seen from the air. From down here it doesn't look to me like it would fool anyone. They just look like badly painted buildings. Maybe from up in the air you would think it was a mountain or something. There are sandbags placed all around them, and the windows are taped to prevent flying glass. You couldn't see in the windows if there was anything to see, which there isn't. They hardly have anything in them because there have been so few shipments from the mainland.

They've taken down all the Christmas lights and holiday decorations so it doesn't even look like Christmas, and it certainly doesn't feel like it.

This year we have soldiers instead of Santas.

The only thing that reminds you that it's Christmas when you're downtown is the Salvation Army people with their kettles and tinkling bells.

We're not even going to have a tree. The trees come from the mainland, and, of course, there are none. Although Mom and I have decorated the house, it doesn't really look like much without a tree.

Mom's really happy about the butcher, though. The butcher really, really loves Mom, so he saves her some of her favorite cuts of meat. He knows how much care and pride Mom puts into preparing a meal. For Christmas he is saving her a nice big leg of lamb. And Mom's going to make twice-baked potatoes, Dad's favorite.

The other thing that makes Mom happy is that she can still get Walter Winchell on the radio. The local radio stations have been off the air since the attack. This is so that the Japanese planes can't follow the radio beams, which seems pretty silly to me. The Japanese were capable of finding Pearl Harbor the first time and, since they've already been here once, I would imagine they know the way without radio beams.

Andy tunes in the police radio and listens to the dispatcher telling the police cars all the suspicious things that have to be investigated. It's really spooky listening to that.

I was going to write Allison today, but I'm afraid of the censors. Dad says they take out anything they think is unacceptable. You have to be especially careful not to say anything about the weather, because they consider that essential information. They cut out any offending words and then reseal the envelope with censor's tape.

I told Mom I didn't think this was a good time to write, because I didn't want to get into any trouble. She said she "wouldn't even dignify that with a response."

At least we can still go to the movies. We decided to see *How Green Was My Valley,* although Andy voted for *Dumbo* (which is about, of all things, a flying elephant. The world is coming apart at the seams, and people are making movies about flying elephants).

I cried from beginning to end. I don't usually cry at movies. I don't know what came over me. Lately I feel real sensitive, and the movie made me think about how much I care about my family. Even Andy was choked up, you could tell.

After the movie we had to turn in our American money and get the new Hawaiian money. The authorities are afraid that if the Japanese invade, they'll take all our money. The new money has HAWAII printed big on both sides. That way the Japanese won't be able to use it. Andy thinks we should all just use Monopoly money.

Naturally we had to stand in line at the bank for forty-five minutes (the line was around the block). We spend half our lives standing in line now. We line up to be immunized for smallpox, and we line up for gasoline rationing coupons. We're only allowed ten gallons of gasoline a month. Dad takes the bus now when he goes into Honolulu, but even taking the bus is a problem. There aren't enough drivers, so sometimes Dad waits so long, he just comes home.

I didn't take my gas mask with me to the movies or to the bank, and Mom and Dad didn't say anything. The masks are such a pain. They weigh about a million pounds and look ridiculous.

Wednesday, December 24, 1941
Oahu, Hawaii

Mom went to a meeting about school. They still
don't know when we're going to resume class, but
it's not going to be where it was. The military still
needs the facilities. When we do go back, we'll be
divided up into smaller groups, classes will be
held in private homes, and the teachers will go
from house to house to save on gas.

Christmas Day, 1941
Oahu, Hawaii

I heard Mom and Kame's aunt talking in the
kitchen while they were preparing dinner. Miss
Kozuke said that they all had to be very careful
because they were Japanese. Their telephone
conversations are being monitored, and the older
Japanese, like Kame's mother, are not wearing
traditional kimonos or sandals because they are
afraid.

When Kame and I came in, they stopped talking about it. Kame's living with her aunt now. Mrs. Arata and the two boys did not come to dinner.

Miss Kozuke brought fresh vegetables from the victory garden she and Kame planted. It's very difficult to get fresh vegetables, so it was a real treat for everyone except Dad. Dad doesn't eat any vegetables except potatoes. He says they're rabbit food.

Kame's aunt was going to prepare sushi, but she was unable to get the ingredients she needed.

She also brought beans that had been soaked in water and cooked the night before. She and Mom ground the beans, pressed them through the cheesecloth, and poured them into wooden bowls. Kame's aunt said that tofu has lots and lots of protein.

Mom showed Miss Kozuke how to make twice-baked potatoes and said they have lots and lots of starch, which made all of us laugh. It was an odd sound, laughter.

At the dinner table Dad stood up to make a toast. I was really taken by surprise. Dad's never done anything like that. But I could see that something was on his mind. Plus, it was the first time I had ever seen Dad take a drink. Even Mom had never had sake before, and Dad tried it and thought it was "wonderful." He had quite a few of those little cups Miss Kozuke brought to serve the sake in.

He held up one of the little cups and said he wanted to make a toast to those who were unable to join us tonight but who he hoped would be able to very soon: Mr. and Mrs. Arata and the two boys.

Then he said he would like to make a toast to someone who will not be able to join us in the future, Mr. Poole.

He had something more he wanted to say, something about Mr. Poole, but he couldn't do it.

After dinner I told Dad that you could see how much his toast meant to Kame and her aunt. And what a nice way it was to begin Christmas dinner. I told him that he always thinks of everything. "If I thought of everything," he said, "we wouldn't be here."

I told him not to be so hard on himself and gave him a big, big, hug. I love to hug Dad; he smells like an ice-cream soda.

Kame and her aunt left pretty early. They wanted to get home before it got dark. Dad, Andy, and I helped Mom in the kitchen.

Dad tapped his fork on the little sake cup and said he had an announcement. I couldn't believe what I was hearing.

I looked at Mom and could see that this time, she knew.

"They want to evacuate as many people from the island as they can," Dad said. Evacuation will help ease the housing and food shortage. Top priority is being given to women and children, especially pregnant women (which Mom more than qualifies for).

"So we're moving," Dad said, just like he always does, only this time it was so different. How long, was all I could think, praying it would be soon.

"The day after tomorrow," Dad said, answering my question without my even having to ask.

"Amber turned out to be right after all," he said. "We just had a little detour. We're moving to San Francisco."

I didn't know what to say. I was so relieved. It was like a bad dream was finally ending.

Isn't it ironic?

The shortest diary I ever kept, and the saddest.

Epilogue

★★★

Lieutenant Lockhart and his wife were divorced in 1943. A year later, by then addicted to painkillers and alcohol, he committed suicide.

Mr. Arata was released from Sand Island in 1942. The family, including Miss Kozuke, was sent to the Jerome Relocation Center in Arkansas. It was impossible to trace anyone besides Kame after that.

In 1949, Kame married and gave birth to Grace a year later. When Grace was fourteen months old, Kame and her husband were killed in a freak automobile accident.

Amber Billows lost track of Kame immediately after December 1941. She spent years trying to find her, finally succeeding (with the help of her father) only in time to learn of Kame's tragic fate.

Amber then located Grace in an orphanage and adopted her. She and her husband (a documentary filmmaker friend of her brother's) brought her back to their Boston home, where Grace grew up. She was the couple's only and much loved child.

Life in America
in 1941

Historical Note

★★★

"A date which will live in infamy." That was how President Roosevelt described December 7, 1941. It was a day no one expected to be different from any other. Instead, the events of that day changed world history.

By 1941, much of the world was already at war. While the Nazis occupied and terrorized most of Europe, Japan was busy with its own imperialist mission in the Far East. In 1937, conflict between Japan and China escalated when Japan captured the city of Nanking and went on to massacre 300,000 Chinese civilians. Although anger at Japan was evident in the world and in the United States, Americans wanted no part of anyone else's war. This country's usual reaction would have been to protect vulnerable China from an aggressively advancing Japan. But during this period of isolationism and fear, the idea of participating in another war was met with apprehension from the American people. From 1935 to 1937, Congress passed three Neutrality Acts designed to keep us out of conflicts by forbidding arms sales and other supports.

Roosevelt was in a bind. Without the backing of the people, all he could do was ask Congress to amend the Neutrality Acts in some way to allow our government to send supplies to our European allies. By 1941, Roosevelt had the Lend-Lease program to give aid to Great Britain. The program allowed America to provide allied nations with defense supplies without engaging their enemies. Roosevelt was inclined to do more. He would have liked to give more to Great Britain in its fight against Germany. He would have liked to contribute American resources and manpower toward this fight and toward China's fight in the East.

Yet in America, there was an air of quiet denial. Only moderately concerned about the problems in Europe, Americans were even less interested in Japan's actions. Detached geographically from these wars, the American people were reluctant to become involved in them physically or financially. Indeed, they were adamant about staying out of it.

So it wasn't until the summer of 1940 that Roosevelt decided to take some steps toward war. When Japan took Indochina from France, it put the Japanese very close strategically to the Philippines, a group of islands in the Pacific ruled by the United States. America began to strategize. While Congress saw to a renewal of America's naval fleet, Roosevelt banned the sale of certain goods to Japan. As far as Japan was concerned, these were acts of aggression, and they would be answered.

Answered they were. Japan, led by Emperor

Hirohito, allied itself with Adolf Hitler's Nazi Germany and Benito Mussolini's Fascist Italy in a pact under which each leader vowed to support the other if any one of them were attacked by the United States. This was the Tripartite Pact. In light of this alliance, Roosevelt tightened America's purse strings and exports even more. His plan was to cut off Japan's war plans at the source. He placed an embargo on all oil, steel, and iron exports to Japan. Great Britain followed suit. What would Japan run on now? What would they build with? How could they continue this war they had started?

In order to seize the resources that they would need to recover momentum in the war, Japan's navy would have to take the Dutch East Indies, along with British Malaysia and the American Philippines — areas extremely rich in raw materials. This would be impossible unless they defeated America's Pacific fleet first. Hideki Tojo, a

Japanese army general who had just become Prime Minister, decided not to hesitate. A surprise attack in the Pacific was in order. The preparations began.

America had long ago made the islands of Hawaii a territory. By 1941, half of the U.S. Naval Fleet was docked in Oahu's Pearl Harbor. It was a strategic move that enabled America to have a military presence in the Pacific. But even as it accomplished this, it opened the door to a risky proximity to Japan and its dreams of total command of the Far East. Pearl Harbor became a target.

Because Japan's attack on America could only be pulled off successfully if it came as a complete surprise, the bombing of Pearl Harbor was perhaps the riskiest military mission in history. Even as Admiral Isoroku Yamamoto laid his plans, diplomats from both Japan and the United States sought a peaceful resolution. And even while all this was happening, American military intelligence had finally broken the codes that revealed the alarming news that Japan was planning surprise attacks somewhere in the Pacific. But when? Where? Would it be the Philippines? Would they dare attack even closer to American soil?

The Japanese sent out warnings. One was sent to American officials in the Pacific after the first part of Japan's mission, sending war ships in the direction of Hawaii, was put into action on November 26. And another was intercepted on its way to Japanese diplomats in Washington, in town to break off any further negotiations with America. It was a long message. By the time it was decoded, it was early Sunday morning in Hawaii — December 7, 1941. It was too late. What had been a dreamy night in the Pacific harbor turned into a nightmarish dawn.

At 7:55 A.M., bombs crashed down, exploding ships on contact. Anyone who could tried to help the others. But it was no use. The surprise attack had worked. By 9:30 A.M., it was over. Eighteen American ships were lost. Over 300 American military planes destroyed. Over 2,400 American lives were lost and 1,178 people were wounded. The next day, President Roosevelt made the report to the rest of the country. And America went to war.

Many popular Sunday afternoon entertainment programs were interrupted when news of the "sneak attack" was broadcast to the American public via radio bulletins. The news sent a shock wave across the nation, uniting it behind the president and effectively ending isolationist sentiments in the country. The United States was gripped by war hysteria. This was especially strong along the Pacific coast of the United States, where residents feared more Japanese attacks.

People who once lived peacefully side by side became paranoid. Communities demanded that the residents of Japanese ancestry be removed from their homes along the coast and relocated in isolated inland areas. Later, President Roosevelt would sign into effect an order for forcible internment of Japanese people in America. It was a dark time in America's history. While we were fighting wars abroad against fascism and imperialism, America was depriving its own citizens of their civil rights.

All around the country, people were driven by fear. The bombing of Pearl Harbor had brought war too close to home. Posters hung everywhere: "Remember Pearl Harbor!" This was the call to arms that kept Americans enthusiastic. Rationing began and victory gardens sprung up as people were encouraged to grow their own food to avoid shortages. The war raged on for nearly four more years. On August 6, America dropped the first atomic bomb on Hiroshima, Japan. On August 9, another was dropped on Nagasaki. On August 14, 1945, Japan surrendered to the Allies. No country has tried to invade America's shores since.

Luxury yachts dropped anchor in the Ala Wai harbor in Honolulu, Hawaii. The palm tree-lined, mountainous island of Oahu was the base for almost half of the American military fleet in 1941.

The streets of Honolulu in December 1940 were decorated with Christmas lights. But in 1941, after the December 7 attack on Pearl Harbor, public festivities for the Christmas holiday were cancelled, and lights and decorations removed because of strict blackout regulations imposed by the American military.

142

In 1941, in retaliation for an American-led embargo on the export of oil, steel, and iron to Japan, Japanese Prime Minister Hideki Tojo, a former army general, sent an armada of four aircraft carriers transporting 350 bombers, Zero fighters, and torpedo planes to attack the American naval and army bases in the U.S. territory of Hawaii. On Sunday, December 7, 1941, the Japanese aircrafts reached their destination at 7:53 A.M.

The commander of one of the four Japanese aircraft carriers, Shokaku, *watches the jets take off to attack Pearl Harbor early in the morning on December 7, 1941. The Kanji inscription on the wall behind the officer is an appeal to the pilots to do their duty.*

143

This photograph was taken by a Japanese pilot during the raid on the island of Oahu, Hawaii. The American battleships moored in Pearl Harbor, called the Bay of Pu'uola in Hawaiian, were attacked by torpedoes and bombs. In this picture, the USS West Virginia was torpedoed, and the Japanese torpedo planes are visible in the right center of the photo. Eight U.S. battleships were destroyed by the Japanese, leaving the American naval presence in the Pacific crippled.

In the above photograph, the USS Arizona lists and sinks after being hit by at least eight Japanese bombs. Over one thousand U.S. servicemen were killed aboard this battleship. American destroyers USS Cassin and USS Downes were also hit while in drydock. Anti-aircraft shells fired from American crafts explode above the destroyed ships. Below, a photograph snapped from an automobile that was traveling alongside Pearl Harbor shows many of the other American ships that were damaged during the raid.

Wheeler Army Airfield, in central Oahu, was the U.S. Army's main fighter base and was heavily attacked during the raid on Pearl Harbor. Of some 140 planes on the ground there—mainly P-40 (as shown in the photo below) and P-36 pursuit planes—nearly two-thirds were destroyed or put out of action. The Japanese pilots set planes afire with machine gun and cannon fire and sent bombers in to wreck them with explosives.

Hickam Army Airfield, which was adjacent to the Pearl Harbor Navy Yard, was also attacked by the Japanese. Many men were killed at Hickam when the Japanese bombed their barracks, and approximately two-thirds of the jets housed in this airstrip were so badly wrecked, they had to be grounded. However, the American planes, such as the B-17E bomber pictured above, that managed to escape damage flew on defensive missions, shooting down Japanese planes.

Hawaiian civilian volunteers formed the Women's Ambulance Service Patrol (WASP's) in 1942, after the sinking of the American ship USS Wasp. *They provided emergency ambulance service throughout the duration of the war.*

The headlines of the Honolulu Star-Bulletin *newspaper scream the news of the December 7 Japanese aerial attack on the American military base at Pearl Harbor, Hawaii.*

Fifteen officers who were killed during the Pearl Harbor raid were laid to rest the following day, December 8, 1941. A marine rifle squad fires volleys over the graves. More than two thousand Americans lost their lives during the attack.

The crew of the USS Ward *were cited for firing the first retaliatory shots on the morning of the Pearl Harbor raid. The crew of this destroyer spotted a Japanese submarine lurking just outside the harbor, fired, and sank it.*

United States President Franklin Delano Roosevelt delivered a speech to Congress on December 8, 1941, following the attack on Hawaii, in which he asked for a formal declaration of war against Japan. Roosevelt favored entering the war earlier, however America's isolationist tendencies prevented him from sending aid to the Allies in Europe. The raid on Pearl Harbor, which Roosevelt called "a date which will live in infamy," gave him ample reason to join the effort to defeat the Axis powers. Below, American servicemen aboard the USS Wichita *listen to President Roosevelt's address to Congress on the radio.*

Following the attack on Pearl Harbor, residents of Hawaii feared the prospect of a food shortage. With a closure imposed on civilian ships running from the mainland, women lined up at the markets and bakeries to buy food and other necessary provisions. Eventually Hawaii created a food stamp rationing system, and residents planted victory gardens.

All civilians and off-duty military personnel were encouraged to evacuate Hawaii during the Second World War, after the raid on Pearl Harbor. Residents of Hawaii had the choice of whether to stay or go, but the wives and children of military employees were forced to leave. Evacuation and air-raid drills were carried out frequently during war times, to ensure preparedness in the case of a second attack.

Two children are shown with their government-issued gas masks. Everyone in Hawaii was given a gas mask, which they had to carry at all times. The American government promised punishment of a fine if civilians were caught without their gas masks. Also, all residents were told to blackout their homes and to build bomb shelters in their yards in case of another attack by the Japanese.

Map of western United States mainland and U.S. territory of Hawaii. Pearl Harbor is shown.

About the Author
✪✪✪

Barry Denenberg is the author of several critically acclaimed books for young readers, including three books in the Dear America series, *When Will This Cruel War Be Over?: The Civil War Diary of Emma Simpson*, which was named an NCSS Notable Children's Trade Book in the Field of Social Studies and a YALSA Quick Pick; *So Far from Home: The Diary of Mary Driscoll, an Irish Mill Girl*; *One Eye Laughing, the Other Weeping: The Diary of Julie Weiss*; and two books in the My Name Is America series, *The Journal of William Thomas Emerson: A Revolutionary War Patriot* and *The Journal of Ben Uchida, Citizen 13559, Mirror Lake Internment Camp*. Praised for his meticulous research, Barry Denenberg has written books about diverse times in American history, from the Civil War to Vietnam.

Denenberg's nonfiction works include *An American Hero: The True Story of Charles A. Lindbergh*, which was named an ALA Best Book for Young Adults, and a New York Public Library Book for the Teen Age; *Voices from Vietnam*, an ALA Best Book for Young Adults, a *Booklist* Editor's Choice, and a New York Public Library Book for the Teen Age; and *All Shook Up: The Life and Death of Elvis Presley*. He lives with his wife and their daughter in Westchester County, New York.

Acknowledgments

✪✪✪

The author would like to thank Kristen Eberle, Kerry McEneny, Daniel Martinez, Janelle Grey Kensmo, Kylie Kovita, Amy Griffin, Beth Levine, Lisa Sandell, Elizabeth Parisi, Chad Beckerman, Manuela Soares, Kate Lapin, Victoria Maher, and Jeanne Hutter.

✪✪✪

Grateful acknowledgment is made for permission to reprint the following:

Cover Portrait: SuperStock

Cover Background: AP/Wide World

Page 142 (top): View of Pearl Harbor, Bishop Museum Archives.
Page 142 (bottom): Christmas in Honolulu, Bishop Museum Archives.
Page 143 (top): Japanese plane, Official U.S. Navy Photograph, now in the collections of the National Archives, Photo #80-G-182249.
Page 143 (bottom): Japanese officer, Official U.S. Navy Photograph, now in the collections of the National Archives, Photo #80-G-182248.
Page 144: Aerial view of attack on Pearl Harbor, U.S. Naval Historical Center Photograph, Photo #NH 50930.
Page 145 (top): U.S.S. *Arizona* under attack, Official U.S. Navy Photograph, now in the collections of the National Archives, Photo #80-G-40056.

Page 145 (bottom): View of Pearl Harbor raid from car window, Official U.S. Navy Photograph, now in the collections of the National Archives, Photo #80-G-33045.

Page 146 (top): Wheeler Field, U.S. Naval Historical Center Photograph, Photo #NH 50473.

Page 146 (bottom): Destroyed aircraft at Wheeler Field, Photograph from the Army Signal Corps Collection in the U.S. National Archives, Photo #SC 134872.

Page 147 (top): B-17E bomber at Hickam Field, Photograph from the Army Signal Corps Collection in the U.S. National Archives, Photo #SC 127002.

Page 147 (bottom): WASP volunteers and ambulance, *Star Bulletin*, November 20, 1943; War Depository Collection, University of Hawaii.

Page 148: Front Page of *Honolulu Star-Bulletin*, December 7, 1941–*Honolulu Advertiser*.

Page 149 (top): Officers' burial, Official U.S. Navy Photograph, now in the collections of the National Archives, Photo #80-G-32854.

Page 149 (bottom): U.S.S. *Ward* gun crew, Official U.S. Navy Photograph, from the collections of the Naval Historical Center, Photo #NH 97446.

Page 150 (top): President Roosevelt's address to Congress, UPI/Acme.

Page 150 (bottom): U.S. servicemen listening to President Roosevelt on the radio, Official U.S. Navy Photograph, now in the collections of the National Archives, Photo #80-G-464088.

Page 151 (top): Food line, *Star Bulletin*, December 8, 1941; War Depository Collection, University of Hawaii.

Page 151 (bottom): Evacuation of Pearl Harbor, *Star Bulletin*, November 5, 1943; War Depository Collection, University of Hawaii.

Page 152 (top): Children with gas masks, from the book *Pearl Harbor Child* by Dorinda Makanaonalani Nicholson, civilian survivor of the attack on Pearl Harbor.

Page 152 (bottom): Map by Jim McMahon.

Other Dear America books
by Barry Denenberg

When Will This Cruel War Be Over?
The Civil War Diary of Emma Simpson

So Far from Home
The Diary of Mary Driscoll, an Irish Mill Girl

One Eye Laughing, the Other Weeping
The Diary of Julie Weiss

My Name Is America books
by Barry Denenberg

The Journal of William Thomas Emerson
A Revolutionary War Patriot

The Journal of Ben Uchida
Citizen 13559, Mirror Lake Internment Camp

Copyright © 2001 by Barry Denenberg
✪✪✪

Library of Congress Cataloging-in-Publication Data
Denenberg, Barry.
Early Sunday Morning: the Pearl harbor diary of Amber Billows/
by Barry Denenberg.--1st ed.
p. cm--(Dear America)
Summary: In her diary, twelve-year old Amber describes moving to Hawaii in
1941 and experiencing the horror of the bombing of Pearl Harbor.
ISBN (paper over board) 0-439-32874-8
[1. Pearl Harbor (Hawaii), Attack on,1941--Fiction. 2. World War, 1939-1945--
Fiction. 3. Hawaii--Fiction. 4. Diaries--Fiction.] I. Title. II. Series.
PZ7.D4135 Ear 2001
[Fic]--dc21

10   9   8   7   6   5   4   01   02   03   04   05

The display type was set in Minister Book.
The text type was set in New Aster.
Book design by Elizabeth B. Parisi
Photo research by Zoe Moffitt

Printed in the U.S.A.   23
First edition, October 2001
✪✪✪